THE NATASHAS

THE
NATASHAS

a novel

YELENA MOSKOVICH

DZANC
BOOKS

DZANC BOOKS

5220 Dexter Ann Arbor Rd.
Ann Arbor, MI 48103
www.dzancbooks.org

Library of Congress Cataloging-in-Publication Data

Names: Moskovich, Yelena, 1984- author.
Title: The Natashas / Yelena Moskovich.
Description: First U.S. edition. | Ann Arbor, MI : Dzanc Books, 2018.
Identifiers: LCCN 2017045114 | ISBN 9781945814488 (softcover)
Subjects: LCSH: Interpersonal relations--Fiction. | Self-realization--Fiction.
Classification: LCC PR9105.9.M67 N38 2018 | DDC 823/.92--dc23
LC record available at https://lccn.loc.gov/2017045114

Originally published as *The Natashas* in the United Kingdom by Serpent's Tail, Copyright © 2016.

First US edition: March 2018
Interior design by Leslie Vedder

Printed in the United States of America

10 9 8 7 6 5 4 3 2 1

ECCE DEUS FORTIOR MI, QUI VENIENS DOMINABITUR MIHI.

BEHOLD A GOD MORE POWERFUL THAN I, WHO

COMES TO RULE OVER ME.

—Dante Alighieri, *A New Life*

"I HAD TO LAUGH LIKE HELL."

—Kurt Vonnegut, *Hocus Pocus*

I

NATASHA IS HER NAME

1

IN THE BOX-SHAPED ROOM, there are no windows, there is no furniture. On the floor, blankets are spread one next to another like beach towels. Some are neatly arranged into rectangles. Others stay bunched like spat-out gum. One girl is sitting on her blanket in a T-shirt and underwear with her arms crossed over her knees. Natasha is her name. She is fifteen.

Another girl is standing against the wall and smoking. She exhales then blows the smoke into the wall as if there were an open window. The smoke crashes like watercolor, then floats back into her face. It seeps into her chopped blonde hair and settles down into her scalp. A fog hovers near her eyes. She is smoking and squinting. Natasha is her name. What a coincidence. She's older than the other girl though. Almost twenty. Maybe.

Next to her, two girls are chitchatting. This and that. The shorter one has a flat face. Her age, hard to say—either too young or too old. Some girls just turn out like that—in the evening glow she's *your angel*, but in a bathroom glare, you'd ask her where her daughter went. Their names? What do you know: Natasha and Natasha.

The one who is sitting in her underwear has tenantless eyes. A redhead walks past and flicks her shoulder. "Perk up," she says.

The redhead's hair is dry as twine, but she's got big lips and a milk-drop nose. This is very pleasing, especially for people who want to look at a woman and see a girl. *How old are you, sweetheart?* "Oh you know, candy-wrappers, hair-bows, goo-goo-ga-ga." Is that a good age for you? *What's your name, sweetheart?* The girl's eyes dart up. "Natasha," she says as if reading an ingredient off a pill box. Is that a good name for you?

The sitting Natasha does not perk up as suggested by the redhead. The redhead Natasha says, "Flowers that don't go for the sun get trampled on," and pushes past the sitting Natasha. She hasn't gone three steps forward when a lanky girl pops up in her path.

"I'm a sunflower." Her hair is greasy. Her neck is long.

"Move it, sunflower," the redhead spits, and just as quickly as she'd popped up, the sunflower bends back against the wall.

The sunflower is twenty-six years old. At first she insisted that she was from Moldova, but we all know girls that tall don't grow in Moldova. That was back when the against-the-wall Natasha had long blonde hair instead of that cropped mess and kept talking about the white rose. Same old story: the foggy town, the stranger with manners, the bus stop, white teeth, white car…and *the white rose*. He picked her out of all the other girls at her school, made her feel like she was the only one. That was years ago. Now she sticks to her wall and smokes and keeps quiet. She doesn't try to bring up the white rose anymore. Well, with her cut-up hair and ashen face, no use in making a fuss. Good thing too, cause there's nothing worse than a Natasha who makes a fuss.

2

By the way, *Sunflower* isn't actually Sunflower's name. It's Natasha. Life's a one-key piano sometimes…

3

On the other side of the room, a girl is blowing on her hand, one nail at a time. She's got baby-blue eyeshadow layered on her eyelids like dust on antique furniture. She blows across her fingertips. She blinks. Baby-blue dust flies from her eyes.

4

Another Natasha pats her blanket looking for her journal. *So many ways to feel ugly...I should make a list!*

She takes the plastic pen into her mouth and bites down.

"*Find a bump on your skin,*" she mumbles.

"*Carefully pick it open,*" she scribbles.

"*Now let all the voices in,*" she concludes.

She looks up from her journal and chews on her pen as if she's teething. A flash crosses her eyes. She takes the pen out of her mouth and pulls the open journal closer to her face.

"*Listen, listen, listen...*" she notes secretly.

She lifts her gaze and circles it around her, keeping the journal close to her chin. Her pen moves across the paper while her head nods at her surroundings.

She writes in a succession of strokes, as if sketching a landscape: "*You're not worth a thing.*"

5

The other girl blows on her nails in rhythm to the moving pen. *Mercedes Red* is the glossy color on each fingernail. We all know why it's the only nail polish she uses. It's the color of the car, that one day, when the door opened and she felt that in the whole world there was no one, no one, no one else like her. The man at the wheel had such a straight smile. She did not have a TV, but was sure he was on it, smiling just like that. She wanted to be on this TV too. He could kiss her on the cheek. He could kiss her on the hand. All his kisses would make her lips and nails flush to match his car. When she told her mother of the stranger and his proposition, her mother lifted her hand high and shook it. *Head in the clouds, this one! No way a man like that would let you step inside such a beautiful vehicle!*

The day she left with him, she asked if he could roll the top down as they drove through the town. He smiled in geometric perfection and said, *Anything for you.* Her small zip-up bag was in the back seat. Together, they drove through her childhood streets as everyone she had grown up with hurried out of their houses and pointed and giggled and tugged at each others' clothes. *If anyone owned a camera in this stupid town, someone would be taking my picture now!* she thought to herself and smiled and waved with her fingertips and ran her fingers through her hair like a movie star.

When she drove past her own house, her mother stepped out with her younger sister and brothers. They all stared with open mouths. The wheels of the car rolled delicately over the layer of gravel on the dirt road. She caught her mother's eye. With the most refined hand gesture she could think of, she flipped a mesh of hair over her shoulder.

She had never, in whole her life, seen such glowing pride in her mother's face. She was so touched that she forgot all about her plan to yell out, *Told you so…!*

Mercedes Red is her color now. Perhaps it always was. What is her name?

Listen, listen…Listen to this girl's breath falling out of her mouth and on to those glossy-tipped fingers.

6

"*Stare at a hair on your thigh*," she mumbles.
"*Try to get out through your eye*," she scribbles.
Her teeth dig into the pen until the plastic starts to dent.

7

In this box-shaped windowless room, all the girls are named Natasha.

II

BÉATRICE

1

BÉATRICE'S ROOM WAS SEPARATE from the rest of the house. It protruded from the roof, giving the troubling perspective to the birds that Béatrice was trapped in an oversized aviary.

At the age of twenty-nine, Béatrice still lived with her family, just outside Paris, on the southeast border of the city. Her sister Emmanuelle, who was one year younger, lived there too. Emmanuelle had a steady boyfriend and was just finishing her residency as a nurse. Béatrice had no boyfriend and sang jazz in small bars. Both sisters lived in their separate ways, waiting for life to break off and become their own.

Their father owned his own business selling oriental rugs and carpeting to a clientele with a taste for luxury and the Far East. He had two boutiques in Paris, one in Saint-Germain and one in Montmartre. Her mother was a home decorator by vocation, but had become a stay-at-home mom to raise the girls. She transferred her home decorating skills into the stylized upbringing of her daughters, where great care was taken in arranging them to fit the house. After her girls had grown up, she had become so accustomed to this kind of work that she continued her upkeep of the house as if raising a third and favorite child.

2

Both mother and father had taken notice of Béatrice's voice at a young age when she still shared a room with her sister, and went around the house with her brushed angel hair, singing Céline Dion and, to their surprise, reaching every note. In middle school, Béatrice discovered Mariah Carey and spent her free time mastering the octave changes and the frequencies of lushness. When Béatrice sang at home, her mother led her around the rooms as if spreading a scent. Her father, however, had an idea. He sat his angel down beside him as he listened to his favorite radio station, the jazz station.

"Listen…listen…" her father said secretly. Béatrice listened.

"You think you can sing like that…"

"Like what?" Béatrice asked.

"Like the woman on the radio," he said, referring to Lena Horne singing "Stormy Weather."

"Dunno." Béatrice shrugged.

"Give it a try, angel…"

Her father paused, trying to contain his excitement.

Béatrice looked up at him. "Okay…" she said cautiously.

Béatrice slowly opened her mouth. The sound began to rise. Her father's eyes lit up.

3

At first, Béatrice tried simply to imitate the classics, Nina Simone, Billie Holiday, Etta James, Peggy Lee…but then, little by little, she found her own swing, texture, and emotional charge.

When it was time for her to go to high school, her father enrolled Béatrice in a private music college. Her mother's contribution was to rearrange the storage space in the attic into a bedroom for Béatrice so that she could sing undisturbed.

4

From that storage space down to the second floor of the house was a steep and narrow stairway of unvarnished wood. It was clear that it would need to be painted. Her mother chose the color, a pale, milky green—it worked well with the egg-white and feather-gray palette of the hallway. It was important to her that colors did not fight.

Her father wedged open the tops of the paint tins, one for himself and one for Béatrice, and together they spent a Sunday morning painting the stairs. Béatrice started with short, stubby strokes as if painting an elephant's toenails. Her father swept his brush generously, and every now and then dabbed Béatrice's elbow with the paint, at which Béatrice frowned, then smiled, then frowned.

Béatrice concentrated so much on the way her brush spread the paint upon the wood that her dad would lean in slowly and blow on her nose.

"If you stay this quiet, I won't know the difference between you and the stairs and I'll paint over you both."

When the stairway was coated twice, her father insisted that three's the charm, or as far as paint goes, you could never be too sure, so they sat down together on Monday night as well and gave it a last coat.

In the end, the stairs seemed to have more paint than they could hold. They were glossy with it, a milky apple green.

"You've made the paint too thick!" her mother exclaimed, tensing her lips and looking back at her husband. He looked away. Into his silence, Béatrice spoke, saying that it was fine, that she did not mind the glossy stairs, in fact she liked them better that way.

With a flicker of pride, her father lifted his hand and placed it on Béatrice's shoulder. She turned her head and looked at him. He looked right back at her and saw then a landscape of dunes.

5

The wind pushed on the trees. Inside the house, Béatrice began to climb the stairs. Her mother put down the laundry basket and walked into the corridor. She saw her daughter rising, one step at a time. As her eyes swept down her daughter's back, she thought she saw Béatrice veering. She imagined her daughter's body flopping down each step like a fish. Her mouth opened and all the air in the house rushed in.

Béatrice heard her gasp and turned her head. She had not known she was being watched. In that pivot her foot stuttered. Béatrice's arms flew upward and grabbed hopelessly at emptiness. Her legs folded and she galloped down the stairs on her tailbone.

6

When Béatrice came back from the hospital, the doctor said she was a lucky girl, no serious damage. She had only broken her hymen.

Emmanuelle hugged her sister very carefully and even lay in bed with her, stringing together lulling questions. Béatrice explained that it wasn't so bad and that all it meant was that she was no longer a virgin. Her sister was at the age where, to understand unlived concepts, vocabulary develops in binary pairs. Emmanuelle slid herself closer to her sister and asked in a gentle voice: "So now you're a whore…"

That night, their father came home with sandpaper. His wife explained to him in emphatic repetition about the stairs that almost broke their daughter's neck. He looked at the waxy steps. They were indeed as sleek as the scream that must have come out of his little angel when she fell down them.

"Don't you realize," his wife repeated, "you almost made her a cripple for life!"

Her father pressed his lips together until his eyes became styrofoam. He spoke softly. "…Her neck is fine…"

His wife rolled her eyes and left the room. All alone, he released his lips, and his eyes began to water.

As Béatrice drifted into sleep, he pressed the grainy paper into the slippery surface and rasped diligently at each step. Béatrice dreamt that she was placing stones one by one in a circle on hot sand. Emmanuelle dreamt that Béatrice died and that the whole family had to watch TV together on the couch and hold her dead body across their laps.

7

When Béatrice reached puberty, her father made two changes: he stopped calling her *his angel* and started asking about *the boys in her class*. As Béatrice's face and body sculpted into a form of enticement, she acquired a new name in the house. *Miss Monroe*. No one can remember if it was her mother or her father who had started it. The name caught on with variations, *Miss Marilyn*, *Miss M*…Emmanuelle was the only one to continue to call her sister "Bee."

One day, however, a variation came out of her sister's mouth. *Miss Playboy*. She swore that she heard it from some boys at school. Béatrice pulled Emmanuelle towards her and demanded, "WHO is *Miss Playboy*…!"

Emmanuelle bit her lip sheepishly. "*You* are, Bee…"

Béatrice's hand stiffened to hit her sister across the face, but before she could swing it up, Emmanuelle was already pressed against her, hugging her tightly and murmuring a faint meow.

8

That was fourteen years ago. Now, Béatrice was twenty-nine.

It was morning. A white September sky. The branches outside Béatrice's window were already almost completely bare. In the place of leaves was a perched bird. Béatrice's eyes opened. She slid her hand beneath the covers and down to her stomach. She moved her hand beneath her pajama top, until it reached her breast, which sat amply atop her ribcage. She let her fingers climb slowly up her breast like feet through a swamp, then drew her fingertip over the tip of her translucent nipple. These were the breasts that made men press their teeth together when looking at her.

She pulled her hand out from under the cover and touched her temple. Her fingers were shaking, sending quivers into her scalp. She took a deep breath. As it went down, part of it caught like wool on a nail. She inhaled once more but her breath kept snagging.

She inhaled deeply through her nose and looked at the dark, flaking wood of the branches outside her window. Her eyes met the perched bird still sitting on its branch. Its head was tucked into its chest and crooked downward, its stiff, marble eye on her. A wind came and swayed the branch. The branch swayed and shook the bird. The bird clamped itself tighter to the branch, but did not change its expression. There was something flaking in Béatrice's throat. It sent a tickle through her and her face contorted, unable to cough nor sneeze.

9

Emmanuelle was still asleep in her room when Béatrice came down the pale green and now well-worn sanded stairway. She shut the bathroom door quietly and turned the water on for a bath. As the tub filled, she peeled her top off and let it drop to the floor. She touched her bare stomach. Then she took off her underwear. The water gushed from the faucet and made the sound of hair being frantically brushed. The scratch in her throat began to spread.

Béatrice found her face in the small mirror above the sink. She aligned her eyes with those in the reflection. With both sets of eyes locked into one another, she closed the gap between her face and the face which was hers in the mirror. The two women touched at the nose. She opened her mouth and sang a mindless *Do-bee do-bee do…* into the mirror.

The voice fogged the mouth of the woman in the mirror.

This was a familiar voice. The jazz voice that she knew to be her own.

Béatrice separated herself from the woman in the mirror and pulled her face back in line with her spine. She lifted her hands to her breasts and held their weight.

Her fingers spread and became firmer. She pressed into the cushion of her breasts. It felt like a rolling pin was sliding up her chest. She pressed further. Her eyelids started to droop.

Her breath rolled up her throat, pushing for an exit. She couldn't tell if she was floating upwards or on the verge of falling down. Static laced around her scalp. The scratch in her throat started to break. It charged out of her mouth. It sprang and unfolded. A word.

"*Polina,*" Béatrice gasped onto the mirror, then dropped her head.

She grabbed the sides of the sink and spat. The cold saliva slid down the sink's edge towards the drain, as if into a large porcelain ear.

In the mirror, the warm breath disappeared into its own reflection.

10

Béatrice felt calm for a moment, as if she had just thrown up. Then she remembered the name she had just pronounced.

"*Polina.*"

She did not know any Polinas. She could not even remember hearing such a name. But Béatrice was more alarmed by the sense of loss she felt than by the word itself. She must have absorbed the name unconsciously, she assured herself. From the radio, for example. Or from a book. Or a song. Or a passerby speaking on the phone. These are names without faces.

She turned off the faucet and stepped into the warmth of the water.

"*Polina,*" She said again.

She took her foot out and stepped back.

"*Polina…Polina…Polina…*" she hiccuped, as she left the bathroom and hurried up the stairs to her room.

11

The telephone was ringing downstairs. Béatrice's mother was in the garden. Emmanuelle was awake and in the bathroom now. Her father had gone out to buy bread. Béatrice stood in her room, dry and dressed, breathing normally now, with no names scratching through her. She listened to the ringing, thinking it would run out at any moment, but another ring surfaced through every interval of silence. She opened her door and went down the stairs. The ring continued, as if building a stairway towards her. She went down to the first floor, turned to the hallway table where the phone was sitting and picked up the receiver. Before she could even say "Hello" a man's voice raced at her in Spanish:

"*Hola Señora, estoy llamando en nombre de <SKO>, que está llevando a cabo esta encuesta sobre satisfacción del cliente con la calidad de la formación proporcionada por este Organismo de Capacitación Registrada…*"

Béatrice tried to cut in several times, but the man's words were chinked together like a metal chain. And yet, somehow, his tone remained pleasant and polite.

"*La encuesta se llevó a cabo para conocer la opinión de los clientes sobre su producto <SKO>. <SKO> utiliza la información que usted nos da como parte de sus procesos de mejora continua para asegurar que ofrece productos de calidad a sus clientes.*"

Just as Béatrice was about to hang up, the voice stopped, like an animal sensing her movement. She held the receiver in midair. The man's voice came out of its hiding place, softened. It spoke with the tone of an earlobe.

"Esto sólo tomará un momento de su tiempo…"

Béatrice kept the receiver away from her face, neither placing it on the stand nor bringing it back to her ear.

"Who is this?" she said.

She could tell that the man was still there, his mouth touching his receiver, but he was not saying one word. Béatrice waited. Her elbow was stiff.

Then, the man's voice pounced through the phone.

"Señora Monroe!"

Béatrice dropped the phone. It bounced on its side, then again on its face, emitting the overlapping beeps of several buttons pressed. It rocked up, then back down on its side and became still. Béatrice picked up the receiver and put it to her ear. It was beeping nervously, having hung itself up during the fall. She placed it back on the stand, then walked up to her room.

With the door closed, she brushed her hair slowly, then pinned it up into a tight chignon.

12

Béatrice went outside. Her mother was in the garden, knees damp with soil.

"Where are you going, *Miss M…?*" said her mother in tone with the tulips.

Béatrice knew the answer to the question but couldn't find its beginning. "…A dress. For Friday…" she mumbled.

"I thought we were going to go together?" The mother gave a playful frown.

Béatrice knew it was her turn to speak. She saw her father's car drive up the road. He parked and hopped out, holding a baguette and a paper bag of pastries.

"Hello, ladies!" he said, looking only at Béatrice.

"*Miss M's* on her way out…" the mother chimed.

"Oh, is she? Where to, *Miss Monroe*…?" the father said.

"…My concert. I need a dress," Béatrice repeated.

"Don't you want to stay for breakfast?" the father said. "I got you a *chausson aux pommes.*"

Béatrice thought about his question. It felt like a room full of empty shoes. Her father waited. Words formed in her head, then melted like ice into puddles on the floor of that room. There was one shoe floating across a puddle on its sole. She remembered what it was she could say.

"No," she told her father.

"All right," the father said and backed up. "You want me to take you into town and drop you off?"

Béatrice paused. She held the feeling of the floating, solitary shoe. It reminded her of the word at her disposal.

"No," Béatrice said firmly.

The wind blew. A strand of hair worked its way out of her chignon. The father lifted his hand to fix it. As his hand approached her temple it changed its mind and laid itself down like a spoon upon Béatrice's shoulder.

"Goodbye then…*Miss Monroe.*"

III
THE HEAD NATASHA OF THE NATASHAS

1

"You smell like a car engine!" a round-faced Natasha says to the nail-painting Natasha.

She has been trying to sleep. She's got white crust in the creases of her lips. It looks like dried milk, but she hasn't had milk for a long time. Not since her grandma asked her to go out and buy a bottle.

"Would you paint your paws in the other corner, *Bozhé moy!*"

Just as the *Mercedes Red* Natasha tries to find a sufficient path of footholes to move to the other side of the room, a metal rummaging is heard. It's coming from the keyhole of the only door in the room. Click and clang and a chain drops like a brass necklace. The door opens and a woman enters.

Her age no one knows. They say she is twice-over a long life in this room.

This is why she is the Head Natasha of the Natashas.

2

The Head Natasha of the Natashas says, "Okay girls, who here has ever had a papaya?"

Another Natasha closes her journal and says, "Oh yeah, I remember. What a shithole situation that was."

For a while afterward, anytime a breeze would blow underneath Sunflower Natasha's loose T-shirt, she would shout, "Baby's coming back!!" Now she knows better than to make such a scene. Although, in private, when the rest of the girls are asleep, and she feels a coolness float across her skin, she'll tuck her chin and say very quietly to herself, "Hello, baby…"

The redhead budges forth.

"None of you know what a pa-pa-ya is," she says.

"I do." Baby-blue jumps in. "It's like…a German guy who has the thing where he insists you play along. Like he's your father."

"*Papa*—ya?"

"*Ich bin dein kleines Mädchen…*"

"*I'm your little girl*," the Natashas chatter in repetition.

The redhead swipes the air with her stiff hands. "You wish. Blood's thicker than water."

"Ha ha!"

"Huh?"

"I mean the Papa-yas all got their own daughters, they don't need *you*."

"She can be his blood daughter and I'll be his *water daughter*…"

"No, no, no, that's not it." A Natasha from the corner walks forth as if carrying the complete truth in her cheeks. "A PAPAYA is when you make a FUSS and you get your eye PAAP'D."

"You mean *popped*."

(This Natasha is just showing off her English accent. She makes her r's into wide a's, so it looks like she's about to yawn every time she says a word with an r in it. Otherwise, her cheekbones are sharp and her eyes deepset like a post-war country.)

3

As you can see, the Natashas get easily excited. The Head Natasha has to raise her hand and jingle the set of heavy keys on the chain for the girls to quiet down.

"Now, now, ladies, PA-PA-YA is a fruit."

The Natashas freeze where they are. They try as hard as they can to understand what the Head Natasha has just said.

"It's smooth and creamy like a mango. But a different shape. Like this." The Head Natasha forms an oval in the air in front of all the other Natashas. "See…" Then she takes the invisible oval with both hands and pries it open in front of the girls. "And inside the seeds are black, like caviar." The Natashas all stare at the empty space between her hands.

The Head Natasha explains to them what a papaya tastes like. It turns out that none of the Natashas have ever tasted a papaya. They listen with great interest. When she's done, the girl with the freshly painted nails taps the Head Natasha on the ankle.

"*Pa-pa-ya?*" she whispers.

The Head Natasha gently smoothes back the girl's hair.

All the Natashas repeat in unison.

"Pa…Pa…Ya…"

"PA…PA…YA."

"PA PA YA."

Their chanting grows and grows as the Head Natasha places her hand on the doorknob, squeezing the handle and turning. The door opens. In the darkness of the frame is a figure of a waiting man.

At first it is hard to tell that it is a man and not just pure darkness. This is because the man is wearing all black, black gloves, black shoes, and a black woolen mask on his head. There are two holes cut out from which his eyes peer. This is how we know it is a man.

The Head Natasha moves to the side, letting the man in. She closes her fingers over the keys she is holding in her palm. The other Natashas are all suddenly upright, facing forward, mutely attentive.

All the girls' shoulders rise as their hands graze up their waists, catching the hems of their shirts and trailing them upward. They peel off the top layer of what they are wearing and let the garments fall to the floor.

Next, their hands twist behind them. These hands slide up their backs to the clasp of their bras. With a drowsy ease the clasps are undone and the bras flinch and fall off. Their breasts stare out at the man.

Next, the girls' hands drool down to their hip bones. Their fingertips dig under the elastic of their underwear. They push at their waistbands until they are nudged off the hips, down, also to the floor.

The girls stand naked now in front of the man. Their skin tones are all faded and blend in with the cement of the walls. Just their nipples stand out like floating eyes, and their pubic hair like illegibly scribbled notes.

The woolen mask on the man's head stretches between the chin and the nose. He is trying to smile. A hot breath exits where his smile is forming.

Listen, listen, listen…

IV
CÉSAR THE ACTOR

1

CÉSAR HADN'T HEARD THIS song since he had left Mexico. It was his mother's favorite. She couldn't help but sing along whenever it was playing. Unfortunately, she was well aware that her own voice had the eerie passion of an epileptic. So usually, she restrained her desire to sing. *Let the singers do the singing, that's God's order.* But on the rare occasions that she heard this song, she would let herself go, and César and his brothers would squirm with embarrassment at the strange, desperate sounds coming out of their mother. Their father would turn to his boys and say calmly, *Some songs pull the sound right out of you, make your voice twist in pain...*

2

The song was about gratitude, actually. "*Gracias a la vida...*" It belonged to Violeta Parra, a Chilean folk singer, a legend of the melancholic melody. She lived and sang as many female legends before her. The type of women who survive famine, and violence, and humiliation, who push themselves forward when abandoned by justice. To all those listening across the radios of Latin America, she was their unbreakable grandmother. And, as such a woman, she sang to their weak spirits, to their thin hope, to their desperate scepticism. Slowly and generously, she testified to the grace of living things.

"*Gracias a la vida...*"

...you have given me so much,

You gave me two eyes, which when I open them,

I can distinguish perfectly between black and white,

And the starry depths of the sky above,

And amongst the masses, the man that I love.

And so you can imagine it was quite a shock to her fan base that, less than a year after she wrote it, Violeta shot herself in the head. Not everybody had known that she composed the song at the end of her turbulent relationship with the famous Swiss flautist, Gilbert Favre.

It was then that the radio listeners began to ask, *So who's this flute-playing boyfriend,* and *Wait, was living a painful activity for her?*

But that was in February of 1967. Nowadays, when the song plays, if it plays, it sings the words as they are. Some know of her story. Others don't. But any given listener may find themselves thinking, *Whoever she was and however she lived, now at least, nothing hurts.*

3

César had no idea what this song from his childhood was now doing on the radio in Paris. It came as it had come in those years to his mother, strange and generous. But now, his mother was not singing along in torment, and his brothers were not making faces behind him, and his father did not lean in and tell them about pain.

Here, the song was filtering through an old stereo system in the corner of the bare office of his telemarketing job. The sound seemed to change the temperature in the room. The air was no longer sourish, but velvety and humid. And as the song finished, he had one clear urge: to sing it to himself, again and again. And so he did, over and over in his head as he worked anxiously to finish the rest of his calls. When his shift was done, he hurried home to his tiny maid's room apartment and found the song on YouTube. It was a fan-made video consisting of a slideshow of photos of Violeta Parra as the audio track played. All the photos which slid across the screen were so different from one another, it seemed like a montage of at least thirty unrelated women. One, gently smiling to herself. Another, with a gaping, strong mouth. Another glancing up suspiciously. Another joking. Another anguished. Another, simply unwashed.

At first, he sang the lines of the songs quietly, his voice careful to stay hidden under the guitar's strum. But soon, his heart took hold of these lyrics like a bull fighter. His voice followed the juts of passion and swung back with a borrowed old pain. He played the song over and over again and sang and sang and sang. Then he closed his computer and sat in silence.

4

César the actor was named after César the boxer, Julio César Chàvez, a six-time world champion from a city not too far away from where César was born in Mexico. The now legendary fighter had what one could call a modest childhood, growing up in an abandoned railway car with nine sisters and brothers, and a father who worked for the railway. As a child, the future legend watched his mother wash and iron other people's clothes and decided that his fists would give her hands a break in this world. Just before he turned seventeen, Julio César moved to Tijuana and began his professional boxing career.

At twenty-two, Chàvez won his first championship and delivered on his promise. He made his mother's eyes glimmer and her hands rub in circles one over the other, and a voice came out of her that he had never heard before, singing, "*DIOS, DIOS, DIOS!*"

The boxer's story was the old tale every poor family in Mexico prayed would become their own. César's family took part in such prayers. They owned a restaurant where his father cooked, his mother cleaned, and he and his brothers took the orders and served the food. César had grown up in this restaurant, in front of a small TV in the corner, whose talk shows and soap operas perforated the sound of the sizzling kitchen and the chewing of the customers.

His father and brothers loved sports, especially boxing and soccer. The older boy, Raul, and the middle, Alonzo, were both meaty. Raul's weight stretched into a thick and firm woven work of muscle, whereas Alonzo's expanded around him, abiding to gravity and the heat. Raul should have been the one named *Julio César* because he was a fighter. Alonzo was the wall, absorbent, pudgy, he could take hits. Raul was the rattlesnake, he'd whip his knuckles so quick your ear would ring all day like a church bell.

César was not very muscular like Raul, nor very meaty like Alonzo, but finely built for strength. He was agile and strong-lunged, which made him a quick runner and a clear speaker. His eyes were thin, wide and peering, lustrous in their gaze. His eyebrows bracketed his eyes frankly. His fine, triangular face was balanced by the weight of those two sleek eyes, and held in place by a nose, which one could not call large, but gave the sense of disproportion due to its wide nostrils. His lips were thin and bland and tended to disappear in the configuration of his face. This earned him the nickname of "the gecko."

Early on, it was clear to César that he was different from his brothers, different from the other boys and men, not because he was shorter, and not because he ran fast, and not because he was called "the gecko," but because César kept a secret pulsation in his heart, which later his parents referred to as the "artist's gene," but which everyone, except for his parents, knew meant *homosexual.*

César himself knew well what the artist's gene meant. He could not deny what he felt for other boys in class, and men in the streets. His fantasies taunted him. Every time he read a book or saw a film, a male character from the story would nest in César's head. He'd whisper sweetly for weeks on end, asking César if he'd like to kiss him, if he'd like to press his body into him, if he'd like to put his hand down his pants and feel around a bit. At school these thoughts left César flushed and trying desperately to adjust himself before the bell rang and he had to get up from his seat.

As he entered his teenage years, he stayed away from boys altogether. The girls accepted César as funny or nice. They never saw him as strange, partly because they were too busy explaining themselves to him. César listened generously to what they liked and what they did not like and who they were and who they were not, agreeing on their behalf.

In this way, César learned to keep all of his needs to himself, holding close vigil against all surfacing desires, trying to catch them before they showed, and stuff them far, far away.

5

César's father had his views and gut reactions to the idea of homosexuality. That word and the web of connotations that went with it somehow did not seem to fit his son. Yes, his boy was different, but in the way that Julio César the boxer was different, the way that men who make history are different. Perhaps he himself once felt the seed of such a difference, the capacity to leave his signature in history, and this is why when he looked at his Julio César he saw so clearly the type of man he could be. The men who make history grow up as boys of difference, he was sure. They are separated and marked by their uniqueness, which has no way of communicating itself in childhood, but is articulated like poetry in adulthood, if given the chance to survive.

It was his mother who had the hardest time with César's *differ-ence*. She expected her husband to set César straight, to make him understand that he couldn't just live his life without making an effort to correct his defect. He had to marry. His best option was the neighbor's girl, Rosa, who often gazed at him with her velvet eyes and brushed her long, thick black hair so carefully in the window of her house. The problem was Rosa's face. No one could say she was disfigured, but her features clashed with each other terribly. When Rosa's parents first heard her sing by accident, they took it as proof of God's mercy that their ugly daughter happened to have a very beautiful voice. The word got out. Too bad little Rosa was extremely shy. The more attention her voice received, the more private she became about it. Sometimes walking home from the store or all alone in her room she would sing lightly to herself. But when the family had company, her parents would pull her out and brag, "Sing something, Rosa...!" Mother, father, and present company would all stare at the girl, who responded to their order with a stubborn silence.

Although César's mother had never heard Rosa sing for herself, she was already imagining what a delicious voice that girl must have. It was a shame to see something like that go to waste. Especially when it was well known that a pristine voice was a herald straight from *Dios*. She secretly hoped that such a voice would one day bless her own, which, despite her best efforts, carried sounds from the depths of the eternally suffering. To think that she could have this voice in her own house, singing God's graces for her through the days. Better than the radio.

The way his mother saw it, it was nothing other than a holy sign that she should have such a peculiar son with "the artist's gene" and right next door there should be such an ugly girl with an angel's voice box.

She knew her two other sons would bring her nothing of value with the women they'd end up marrying. She could already see what kind of woman her eldest Raul would choose. He'd somehow find himself a *gringa* blonde, a thin one, who was perhaps new to the culture. He could be very charming, Raul, can't blame the *gringa*. His jawline and strong cheekbones alone would fool any one of those white women. And even when his aggressiveness started to show, it always came out with a bit of magic. His jealousy could be utterly hypnotizing. *God help those gullible women*, the mother thought, *Dios, Dios, keep them away from my house.*

It wouldn't be until after the wedding night that Raul would give his *gringa* her first slap across the face. Then, even if the girl sang a little, her song would be slapped out of her, year by year. César's mother frowned at the thought of having a pouting, flimsy blonde hanging around the house.

As for her other son, Alonzo, he would end up with one of those older women who would be settling for any man to call her own. Alonzo, like Raul, had that strain of violence in him as well. But because he was not as handsome as Raul, it was harder for him to get away with such outbursts, as his aggression was just not nearly as elegant as his brother's. Their mother was sure he would become more and more clumsy over his married years, and she'd have to have a daughter-in-law with black eyes or missing teeth.

This aging wife would become sad and introverted, and this would show especially in her chores. Most importantly though, she would make awful conversation. And to think that she would most likely have to watch her telenovelas with this woman.

César was her only hope. He had just the right soft melancholia to win over Rosa's trust and make her share that delicious voice. If only César could stop spending so much time doing impersonations of all the telenovela characters on TV, perhaps he could get Rosa's attention.

6

"And who do we have here…" his father would ask César when the restaurant had a slow moment.

"*No me toques!*" César cried out, smoothing his trembling fingers over his hairline with theatrical extravagance as he mimicked Estefania, the young beauty who realizes her husband is in fact her sister's murderer.

César's father would smile and after a moment, he'd say, "…Do another…"

"*Cállate la boca, Doctor.*"

"Shut your mouth, Doctor," copying the newly widowed Laura's attack on Arturo, the high-class surgeon who had reconstructed his own face to avoid prison.

"…Do another…"

"*Esto no es amor…esto es un crimen!*"

"This isn't love…this is a criiiiiiime!" César roared, like Doña Carlota confronting the barely legal Alba about her relations with her uncle.

Although César's mother was a bit embarrassed at how well her son managed to portray these women, her discomfort was always overcome by her immediate entertainment. The father listened with a proud smile, patiently waiting for the next installment.

This made his brothers snort secretly.

"You think you're some *star* now…" Alonzo would whisper to César.

Raul waited until his father left the room, then came up behind César and slapped him between his legs.

"This here's the biggest pussy in all of Mexico!"

7

César el actor his brothers called him in front of their father, who took this as a sign that the brothers respected each other. *César el gecko* his brothers called him in the streets, to show the other kids

that they did not share César's strangeness. And on very special occasions, usually in the darkness of their shared bedroom, while César
was asleep, the brothers took turns whispering into his smooth, boyish ear, *César la puta*. Beneath his closed eyelids, César's eyes rolled
back and forth as his brothers quietly chanted *puta, puta, puta*, pulling their penises out and circling them above César's sleeping face.

8

When César announced he would not be staying at the family restaurant, nor would he be going to secondary school, nor would he be
looking for other work around town, his mother's face went white. "But
what, then, will you do?" she said, looking at her husband for support.

"I'll be moving to Paris," César said. "I'm going to become a
European actor."

His mother's face fell. His father, however, nodded and smiled
quietly. This was the first step a boy of difference had to take to become a man of significance.

On the day of César's departure, his brothers hugged him in
front of their father. Alonzo squeezed him too tight and Raul hit his
back twice. His mother asked what this meant for his marriage plans.

As he placed his suitcase in the trunk of the car, he looked up and
happened to catch the velvet eyes of his neighbor Rosa who was standing in the window with her long, dark hair brushed around her face.

César lifted his hand and waved to Rosa. Perhaps it looked as
if he was shielding his eyes from the sun. She didn't wave back. The
corners of her eyes pinched and her cheeks began to hollow.

9

That was years ago. A different continent. A different life.

Now in Paris, César had finished acting school, got an agent,
learned French, and currently worked as a telemarketer in a little

office that smelled of cardboard, off Rue de la Paix near the Opéra Garnier. He made calls in French and Spanish for various surveys. The French surveys were local and the Spanish were usually for off-shore companies in Spain and Latin America. This was of course a part-time job, but it at least provided a steady workload. He supplemented these wages with ever-changing projects and small jobs he found on online ads. Among these were hanging posters in the metro with a bucket of sticky soap and large folded squares, pasted together upon the wall. He tried cleaning rental apartments for a while, but felt his lungs growing infested with those cleaning sprays. The easy option was teaching private Spanish classes. He had done this in the beginning, but the smooth-skinned French kids with their immaculately shaped upper lips spoke his language like heirs to some throne asking about the local prostitutes.

There was something about telemarketing that he liked best. And even his boss had to admit he was good at it. His only problem was that sometimes he would mix up the surveys and call a French household with a Spanish survey or vice versa. But usually he could catch himself and get back on track, and even sometimes endear his angered listener.

Even if he had to spend his daylight hours in a little office that smelled of cardboard, making endless calls for various surveys, he could have his cell phone next to him in case his agent had an immediate job for him. All his agent's calls were for immediate jobs. Over the years César had scampered to various auditions for commercials and walk-on roles, but had yet to land one. However, his agent had a potent way of encouraging César. Every time César would build up the courage to tell his agent that things were not working out between them, he would leave the conversation somehow more excited than ever about his future with such professional representation.

And so the patient cell phone was to him like a sacred statue of Maria Magdalena, purified by her devotion. Looking at his cell phone now, César suddenly remembered his mother mentioning to him how Maria Magdalena was cleansed of her seven demons by Jesus. His mother's tone had hinted that César too might be in need of demon-cleansing.

10

César saw each telemarketing call as an acting exercise. There were infinite nuances with which one could present the same script. Yet he was not interested in caricatures, false accents, vocal pretenses. His technique was rather to stay wholly himself, and pull out from his own depths, like a white hair from a bowl of milk, the traits needed for his character.

At first he made calls as the characters from the telenovelas of his childhood. He was tempted to choose the female characters, as he felt he did those better. But in order to sound more natural on the phone, he decided to work on the male ones. How would Enrique, the disinherited deviant son, offer a discount rate for his customer's next purchase? How would Federico, the pharmaceutical company mongrel, insist on a few moments of their time? Then, little by little, César got to developing his own characters. Pablo Ruiz, the car thief. Juan-Miguel Santos, the hothead. Andres Sepúlveda, the Chilean melancholic. And so on.

11

That afternoon he had been Juan-Miguel the hothead, which was the most tiring as he had to let his blood boil while remaining calm and vocally personable. Of the hundred and thirty calls he had made, about one-third picked up the phone. And of that third, about one-third let him get past the first sentence before hanging up. And of that third, about one-third gave him a chance at a second sentence. And of that third, about one-third actually spoke to him.

Juan-Miguel the hothead did not do well with these percentages. But what stewed Juan-Miguel's anger the most was a woman's silence. César discovered this character trait the day he discovered the character himself. On one of his calls, a woman picked up the phone without answering. He heard a baby screaming in the background and another child, a boy of five or six, closer in range, repeating, "...*El bebé está llorando*...The baby's crying..." The woman held the receiver in her hand, breathing gradually, as the small boy's voice paced in the background. César rephrased his introduction and gave ample time for the woman to either speak or hang up. But the only sound César heard was the small boy's voice, *bebé llorando*...

As César took a breath, he prepared a soft, empathetic tone towards this seemingly exhausted mother. However, when he exhaled to speak, César realized the back of his teeth were tightly locked. And then he said, "*Puta.*"

It was the first time César had uttered this word, and in the way his brothers would have said it. When he heard himself on the phone, he could barely recognize his own voice. It had to be somebody else. It had to be a new character rising. He called him Juan-Miguel. And he was a hothead. So it was understandable that the days when Juan-Miguel took the wheel were particularly draining. Especially when a woman answered the phone, but did not respond sufficiently to Juan-Miguel's demands.

12

On this day, César had spent all afternoon as Juan-Miguel, so when his shift ended, he hung up the last call physically exhausted. He packed up his stuff in silence and walked his usual route up to the Opéra metro. In autumn, the sun starts setting just as everyone decides to take the metro all at once. They drain out of the boutiques and apartment buildings and into the entryways of the metro like rainwater into a sewer. César found himself a small clearing against the wall of the bank on the corner and let the people weave around him. He needed to stand for a bit.

As he leaned his back against the wheat-stone exterior of the bank, he looked up at the opera house in front of him. Against the setting sun, the building looked like a hero emerging from a low cloud of human destruction. The sight exalted César: a single man against a lost civilization. The hero survives. The hero rises to the surface like an ancient continent breaking through the skin of the ocean. Glorious. Alone. There was something romantic to César about this sort of solitude, a product of external destruction and internal survival.

Standing to the side, the full perspective of the opera house leaned into his gaze. At the top left corner of the building, he saw the seven-foot gilt bronze statue of a woman. "Melody" was her name. Her right hand reached out and her palm opened hesitantly to the bare sky, as if to tell someone out there to stop, or maybe even to cover her face. Her gesture, like her presence, seemed to go unnoticed by the daily crowds of people fumbling around beneath. If she is asking for mercy, César contemplated, she should take her hand away from her eyes.

Two androgynous figures sat at her side, each looking their own way. In her hand, César knew that the woman should be holding a lyre. But from where he was standing, it looked like she was holding an infant under her arm, a brutish, biblical fistful.

César traced his eyes back to that plump golden hand against the spread of sky. He found his attention sliding down her muscular forearm, over the curve of her shoulder, around her broad breasts, down her metal belly and sweeping up to those fingers holding the golden infant like a runt pig to the slaughterhouse. *No, it's a lyre*, César reminded himself.

A crown of spikes encircled the statue's forehead. Two sharp-tipped wings broke out of her back. The bruising skyline gave her a somber glow. The breath in César's chest kept stretching and stretching as he looked over the bronze woman's body. His eyes went to the infant. Then to the plump golden palm. Then back to the infant. Who was now a lyre. Who was now a pig. Who was now music. Her bronze fingertips were playing the wind.

13

Standing there, staring at the statue, César felt a doubting darkness begin to spread within him like an ink droplet in a glass of water. A list of things he didn't like about himself came to mind. His flat, wide nostrils. His slit-thin eyes. The brackets his brows made when he was thinking. Once the surface was picked, the darkness reached beneath. There was something wrong with him, something strange, uncomfortable, underdeveloped, *Der's sumting about you dat make me wanna vomit*, came his brother Raul's voice.

I'm an actor, César took hold of himself. *I'm an uncomfortable, ugly guy, but that's okay, cause I'm an actor. There's a casting agent somewhere out there looking at my photo right now and saying, this guy's perfect!*

César was almost smiling now. He could always count on this kind of pep talk. Nothing mattered if he could just remind himself that he was an actor. Already he felt much better. And with his lifting spirits, his eyes rose too. But no sooner had they reached the skyline than they settled on the plump bronze hand of Melody.

The sight of her metallic palm touched him with a coldness. He couldn't look away. It went deeper than before. Oily words reached between every crevice of his body, echoing between bone and muscle, between joint and nerve, between organ and organ.

You're not worth a thing.

14

In an attempt to get away from these feelings, César began to walk home. He took his familiar route, which was long but pleasant, consisting of a couple of shortcuts seamed together with the classic boulevards where one could indulge in the beauty of the city. César walked without paying much attention to the road, letting his eyes wander about him and airing out his head.

He took in the lace outlines of the Haussmann buildings and street-level shops with names written in that wartime font. He passed by the steam of bakeries, lingering on the scent of rising dough crisping at the surface. He glanced at the candle-white mannequins in the store windows, the women wearing draping chemises and tailored leather, the men, posed like strolling villains, but all with no facial features so that their heads were oversized eyes without pupils. César observed small dogs on leashes pedaling their short legs to keep up with their owners. He saw children walking hand in hand with their parents, telling them about their days with saturated voices unable to find the right volume.

César began to enjoy the walk. He wasn't thinking of anything anymore. Just walking. Just looking. Just listening. It wasn't until he was a third of the way home that he noticed a certain figure within his view. A woman. A woman directly in front of him. How long had he been walking behind the same woman? Maybe all the way from the opera house. How his route home had managed to align so perfectly with someone else's, he had no idea, but the woman did not seem to have noticed him.

He listened to the click of her heels and watched the wavering hem of her thin, mauve coat and the swing of her heavy, dark hair upon her back. His legs felt strange. He no longer knew if he had always walked like this, or if he was copying her walk. He tried to adjust his tempo, change the weight of his step, but he couldn't find his own rhythm. No use in overthinking it, César told himself, and gave in to the unfamiliar footsteps he was taking.

But as César walked on, he realized what was bothering him. He was no longer coincidentally walking the same path as someone else. As he looked around, he realized that he had trailed off his path home. He was following her. And what's more, he was trying to get her to notice. His shoes were stamping against the ground. They felt like bare knuckles rapping on a wooden door. But still the woman seemed oblivious to him.

What if I were not César... What if I were Pablo Ruiz the car thief? César thought. Then he realized this woman had no purse. And the way her coat fluttered, its pockets had to be weightless. The woman's posture was very straight, but the simplicity of the mauve coat left César to assume she was not wealthy. *Nothing to steal, Pablo...*

"Well then...what if I were Juan-Miguel the hothead." The thought immediately bounced in. *Juan-Miguel don giv a shit bout money...*

15

The woman took a turn off the main street into a smaller street, still looking directly in front of her. César followed. The street was lined with out-of-business shops and apartments that seemed to have been abandoned in a hurry.

This narrow street led into another, shorter one. At the end of it, the woman turned left abruptly and continued up a street filled with parked cars, squeezed in bumper to bumper. From the look of it, the street seemed to come to a dead end, yet as they came closer, an alleyway appeared on the right. The woman went up into it. César followed behind.

The alleyway opened onto a paved road hemmed in by rows of silent buildings arching up a slight hill. César glanced up the hill, above the buildings .and saw a moonless evening sky. *When did it get so dark?* he wondered. A street lamp diffused a netting of light which caught the silver wheel rims of the parked cars and the waxy leaves of the potted plants slumped over empty balconies.

They walked on. Above them, the sky was grainy and woolen. The woman's heavy hair rose and fainted with each step. César was so close to her that he could feel the warmth from her body. He suddenly didn't want to be following this woman anymore. Above all, he didn't want to be this close to her. He tried to pull away, but the energy of Juan-Miguel the hothead held him in place.

I...don't want to get any closer, César the gecko said to Juan-Miguel.

This upset Juan-Miguel. He pushed on the soles of César's feet, which made César step even closer to the woman.

A few strands of her hair brushed lightly against the tip of César's nose. It was such a gentle, minute feeling, it made César want to close his eyes like a baby lulled to sleep. Then leaning too far, the tip of César's shoe wedged into the woman's heel. César pulled his hips back and his other foot down to keep himself from falling. The woman had stopped. She was turning around towards César.

There was her shoulder.

There was her ear.

There was her cheek.

There was her eye.

V

MISS MONROE

1

THEY WERE STUDYING THE French Revolution in middle school when Béatrice's breasts began to grow. At the time most of the boys her age didn't bother her. They were more befuddled by the metamorphosis which had turned the body of a schoolmate into that of the woman who visited their bed at night and their shower in the morning and hid beneath their mattress during the day.

There was one exception. A tall boy with a square face started whispering "sex-bomb Béa" at her in the hallways. He was always accompanied by two other boys with constipated smirks. This went on for weeks until the day came when, instead of walking past them with her eyes averted, she stopped and asked, "What do you want?"

The tall, square-faced boy parted his lips and emitted a husky sound to let her know he was ready to speak. He turned his fingers over one another inside his pocket, and pulled out a 100-franc note like a piece of wet clothing from a tub. It had the head of Eugène Delacroix printed on it. His eyes on the wrinkled paper darted forward in acute concentration, as if in the midst of painting the nipple of the bare-breasted woman holding the French flag in *Liberty Leading the People*.

Right there, in the middle of the hallway, with the note in hand and his boys at his side, the tall, square-faced boy began to sing the anthem of his country. *"ALLEZ ENFANTS DE LA PATRIE..."* By the second phrase, the other boys were proudly singing together: "LE JOUR DE GLOIRE EST ARRIVÉ! ..." A kid in the distance hooted and a couple more joined in the song. Soon the others were clapping and cheering—for no reason other than it felt nice to be included.

As the French anthem boomed down the hallway, the tall boy thrust the note into Béatrice's face, so close that she could smell the staleness of the paper. She swatted it away, but the boy quickly snapped it back into her face, this time pressing it to her nose. She raised both hands up in defense, but they were immediately grabbed by the other boys, who were no longer shy teenagers, but empowered patriots.

They twisted her arms behind her back as the tall boy covered her mouth with Eugène Delacroix's face. He pushed the note until it flattened her lips and crumbled into the crevice between her teeth. Her saliva took in the fermented taste of the paper. She tried to breathe out, but found herself choking. Her eyes opened frantically. There were other hands on her now.

One hand pinched her nipple, then let go. Another squeezed her breast until she thought it would bruise. A third jumped from one breast to the other in a grappling frenzy.

It did not take long for the hallway to fill with a flood of voices chanting the anthem. Certain kids stretched out their arms in dramatic angles to each other while singing, others snuck up behind a friend and chopped at the back of their neck, joyfully proclaiming, "Guillotine!" at which their friend would roll their head to the side and let their tongue fall out of their mouth. A sort of festival built around the hyperventilating Béatrice. Just below her gaze, the hands kept grabbing and kneading at her breasts. The more they did it the further away she drifted from what was happening to her. She felt very light just then, thinner than the paper note stuffed into her mouth.

Her skin turned so pale that even the square-faced boy became concerned. Still chewing at her breast with his free hand, he gave Béatrice a bit of worldly advice.

"Breathe through your nose, *Miss Playboy...*" he said.

Finally a teacher came into the hallway, her face curdled with anger at the noise. As she looked around, her expression quickly changed. A proud smile began to grow on her face at the sight of all those young boys and girls so passionately singing their country's anthem.

2

That was the day her father asked her about *the boys in her class* when she got home from school. He stood observing his daughter's curious silence.

"...You okay, honey?" he asked gently.

Béatrice looked at her father but let her eyes glaze over.

"*Do-bee do-bee doo...*" she sang lightly.

Her father lifted his hand towards his daughter's face, extending his forefinger. He traced an evaporating line around her chin.

"Miss Monroe," he whispered and smiled.

3

After high school, Béatrice surprised everyone by failing all of her entrance exams into the top music conservatories. Her sister Emmanuelle was shocked as well, but somehow had the feeling all along that Béatrice was bound for this disappointment, and even more so, that this was only the beginning. Emmanuelle sensed this not because she wished her sister harm, but because she seemed to be the only one in the family to see that her beautiful sister was dying in a way, dying faster than the eye could see. This is perhaps what made Béatrice such a feast for the fantasies of others.

Béatrice cried in her father's arms as he assured her that failing these exams was not the end of the world. "No," Béatrice replied, "it's the beginning of a world I don't want to live in!"

"Miss Monroe," her father said gently, "it's up to you…you can live in whatever world you want…"

This phrase kept coming back to Béatrice. It told her again and again that she was lost. She wished her father could have assured her that no matter what her failures, she would go on living in the same world as everyone else, in the same world where all those jazz women sing in turns, where people win Nobel Prizes and flowers grow symmetrically in gardens.

But her father did not assure her of this. He gave her a set of words that reminded her that she did not live in the same world where brilliant things happened, because she lacked brilliance. She lived in another world, the world she *deserved*, because she was without the capacity of courage or ingenuity required to *want* brilliance.

One day soon after her results had come through, her father found his Marilyn Monroe crouched in the corner of her room, her chignon undone, meshes of blonde hair swinging into her gasping cheeks as her hands grabbed at her own face. He ran to her side and began stroking her back, repeating in a low, loving voice, "Breathe through your nose, honey, breathe through your nose…"

4

For a time, she decided not to decide. She stayed in her room, fogged with an expansive feeling of meaninglessness. She did not speak. She did not sing. She opened her mouth to breathe but exerted no energy beyond that.

Her father came home with a pair of oversized, cushioned headphones. He placed them on his daughter's ears, then plugged the cord into the computer. He pulled up Nina Simone, slowly adjusting the sound like running the right temperature for a bath. When the volume was right, he left the selection on repeat. Béatrice lay detached, with each headphone like a child's hand cupped over her ears. Days passed like this. Maybe years. Many women sang to her of many pains and many joys.

And eventually, music came back to Béatrice.

5

Music came back to Béatrice as armor, as a revolt. She sang. In her room, down the stairs, in the shower, in the kitchen, in the garden. Her father watched her graze on music throughout the house, then cork herself in her room for hours at a time, perfecting, tuning, waxing a shine onto those notes. His listless teenager evaporated like a magic trick and through the smoke a woman emerged with her blonde hair brushed up into a neat chignon, revealing two cold ears. This woman sang like the child he once knew, but no longer in a borrowed voice.

With her father's persistent encouragement, she got in touch with bars and restaurants needing a jazz singer, and she started to sing in the evenings, small concerts for couples sipping wine or twirling linguine around their forks. These turned into steady jazz gigs, and then a regular booking at a bigger bar near the Gare de l'Est. Here, the trains rummaged beneath the floor of the bar and made the furniture hum along with Béatrice as she sang.

6

It was for this very gig that Béatrice needed a dress. She walked out of the central metro onto the boulevard. She passed several stores, but her resolve to find a dress was already losing its momentum. The streets were filled with Saturday morning shoppers. A woman with a stroller stopped abruptly and yelled, "Constance!" A little feather-haired girl ahead turned around and wobbled back to her mother.

A man in a business suit leaned against a wall and smoked a cigarette with his flat cell phone pressed into his ear like a shell.

"Pierre." "Monsieur Levalois."

Then he pulled it away, shaking his head with a grimace.

A girl in tight, bleached jeans shouted a name into the crowd. Her nails were painted a marble blue. "Baptiste!"

"Julie." "Fred." "Anne-So."

A stiff plastic bag was being adjusted in someone's hand.

"Pardon. Pardon. Pardon."

"Anaïs." "Ludovic."

"Madame, Madame."

"Juju." "Sophie" "Toi!"

"Sofia, Sofia."

"*Ya?*"

"Yvette." "Pavla..."

"*Ya?*"

"Viktoria."

"Olena."

"Salomeya!"

"*Ya? Da?*"

"Hello, hello."

"Who is this?"

7

Béatrice pulled the glass door of a small shop closed behind her. The music in the boutique buzzed gently as if it were being played from between the walls. The sound went in and out of focus like a wavering radio channel. A guitar strum. A voice dipped in, a woman. Maybe a flower behind her ear. Maybe her hips clocked from side to side.

The static pushed apart the chords of the guitar and swallowed the voice of the female singer. For a moment there was only white noise, which matched the walls. Then the voice emerged and the chords from the guitar in the background seemed to caress the singer's hair, until her voice calmed down and disappeared back into the static.

The white wall was lined with two rows of white shelves on each side. The shelves were empty. In the oblong space in the middle of the boutique was a rack of clothes. At the back of the shop a doorway was covered by a heavy green curtain hung on wooden rings across a metal bar.

In front of the curtain was a small counter with the cash register. The shopkeeper sat on a stool, looking through an open notebook, adding up numbers. Her hair was dark and heavy, parted in the middle. She did not seem to mind the broken music, perhaps she even kept the radio deliberately between channels.

Béatrice felt that the woman was sure she wouldn't buy anything, so she felt obliged to reach towards the rack and start flipping through the clothes to defend herself. The woman looked up. "Bonjour," she said with a rolled r. Her tan skin had an ashen tone. Her lips were full and dry.

The woman's cheekbones sloped in a way that made Béatrice think that she had lost her watch or that she couldn't have children. But the pupils of her eyes were strong and rimmed with gold.

"Can I help you?" the woman asked. Her accent made the French words sound like they were traveling on a wooden cart.

"I'm looking for a dress," Béatrice answered. She didn't want any help, but the woman's glare made her feel that she had to ask for it.

"All the clothes on the rack are on sale," the woman said.

Béatrice looked around her. The clothes on the rack were the only items in the store, so she continued to page through them. All the garments looked tired, slumped from the hanger's pinch or prod. A pale red cotton dress, then a polyester chemise with a tie at the collar. A pair of dark jeans. The same cotton dress in a broccoli green, then cleaning-liquid blue. Who were these clothes for?

"If you want to try something on…" The shopkeeper did not bother to finish her sentence.

Between another pair of light blue jeans and a wide-necked cream shirt was a long garment of sturdy black lace. Béatrice pulled a corner out. It was a thin deflated arm. She continued to pull. A long dress emerged. It hung to the floor, and rose up to the neck, with full-length sleeves limp at each side. Béatrice pulled out the dress and held it in front of her. It could have been the shed skin of a long, black reptile.

"Very nice," the woman said. "Like a movie star. You want to try it on?"

Béatrice realized her head was nodding, maybe to the music, maybe to the woman's question. The woman got up from her seat sleepily and walked over to Béatrice, then led her to the green curtain and pulled it open.

"Through here."

Béatrice stepped into a dim, damp space which felt like a stone's stomach. The woman clicked on a lamp clamped to a full-length mirror leaning against a stack of boxes. A chair lay on its back on top of another stack. A fold-out table held what appeared to be a sewing machine, covered by a thin, red woolen shawl with blooming white roses printed on it. Next to the machine was a plastic container full of various buttons and a couple of spools of thread.

"Don't mind the stock. Going out of business…"

The woman lingered at the shawl, tracing her finger over a white rose petal. Then she looked over at Béatrice and pointed to the mirror.

"You can look at yourself there," she said.

The woman left through the doorway and pulled the curtain closed behind her. The lamp gave streaks of glare onto the mirror. In the reflection, Béatrice saw a figure holding a black lace dress, but the woman was in a fogged room, separated by translucent slices of light like onion skin. She took her shoes off first.

8

Béatrice stood in front of the mirror with the skin of the black lizard on her. She looked beautiful and dramatic with her collarbone against the lace. The muscles in her stomach clenched, pulling her up taller. This tautness reminded her of a very specific feeling, yet she could not place it. Perhaps it was a romantic feeling, she thought. Like sharing a secret with someone.

But as she continued to investigate this strange feeling, it started to turn sour. There were guitar strums rising in her memory. Then the face of a boy came. The only boy she could say she had ever dated. They had met at the music high school. He played jazz on his guitar day and night, would even fall asleep holding the guitar across his stomach. He was brilliant; it was obvious to teachers and students alike. Béatrice felt privately exhilarated being a part of such undisputed respect. When he touched Béatrice, he touched her almost the way he touched his guitar, which made Béatrice in turn feel like she was, at least in that moment, a bit brilliant too.

Near the end of their studies, he had composed a piece for her. He called it "Keep This Angel Mine," borrowing from Blues and even Sinatra. When he played it on his guitar for her, she imagined a world full of glass bodies with nothing but light in them, like walking lanterns. As he played, he had his own thoughts. He closed his eyes, strummed those strings, and imagined Béatrice's breasts rising and falling as she held his penis in her mouth. When the tempo quickened towards the end, he felt his palm touch her blonde scalp and press down, as *his angel* sucked his soul from him.

After graduation, when Béatrice had failed all her exams, he of course did brilliantly and went straight to New York to fulfill his destiny as a musician of importance for this generation. They broke up. Béatrice expected to go into a sort of mourning, to miss him terribly and pout the way her sister did when her boyfriend went out of town for a weekend. To her surprise, when the boy finally left, his absence produced no physical yearning in her. Quite the opposite, thinking of his face, his body, his voice in his remoteness made her feel embarrassed, at times even humiliated. She did not understand why she couldn't experience the enchanted sadness her sister expressed on a regular basis.

As time went by, she began to realize that they had shared no private complicity at all. Together, they had merely participated in the myth that brilliant boys are noble beings. She felt degraded now to remember him, to remember how she kissed his pinkish penis with so much dedication and how terrified she was to be touched and to be left untouched by the privilege of his hands.

Béatrice spent a lot of time alone after that. Eventually she did start seeing other men. Or it would be more accurate to say, other men saw her. They were mostly the ones she happened to meet through the jazz world, bass players, piano players, men who would accompany her on her gigs. Each "relationship" would last about four weeks and usually the men would get tired of her bouts of silence or uncommunicative nature. (*Even those breasts weren't worth such a hassle.*)

The men couldn't pinpoint it, but it boiled down to the same thing. "Such a shame, with a body like that, the girl's *not all there*."

9

Béatrice blinked firmly and pushed the memory of him away. She drew her attention back to the mirror, concentrating on her reflection.

She turned to one side. Then to the other. She smoothed back her blonde hair with her fingertips. She did look beautiful. She could believe it just now. She heard the radio rise again. The static covered the singer with its fur and the song went on.

On the other side of the curtain, she heard the shop door open and close. Then the sound of heels came in her direction. They clicked one by one, then stopped. Within arm's reach of the curtain, Béatrice guessed.

"Bonjour," she heard the shopkeeper say. Her voice had softened. She spoke with care.

"Bonjour," she heard the other woman say. Her tone was different—neither high nor low, neither husky nor metallic, but matter-of-fact. She, too, had an accent, but much lighter. From where, Béatrice couldn't tell. The music from the radio broke through the static again and Béatrice heard the word "vida" flow from the mouth of the singer like seaweed. The guitar streamed through her voice.

The singer and the guitar drowned out the voices of the two women, who continued their conversation. Béatrice leaned in towards the curtain, but she still couldn't make out the women's words. Maybe they spoke in a different language. Maybe each in her own language. Maybe they were helping each other count to ten. Who knows. Béatrice listened intently.

"*Vida,*" the singer flushed over their words.

Béatrice listened closer.

"*Qué…anto…*"

"*Oché…yoss…*"

"*Idos…*"

She could only hear flakes of the music.

"*Vida*" again.

"*Ala…yenso…*"

"*Outa…qué…*"

Then Béatrice heard the shopkeeper say the one word that couldn't have been clearer.

"Polina."

VI

MY MAN

1

...THERE WAS HER CHEEK.

...There was her eye.

"¿Por qué me estás siguiendo?"

"Why are you following me?" the woman asked César in perfect Spanish.

Her black hair crawled loose from behind her ear and dropped down over her cheek. At the edge of each of her almost-violet eyes the skin was pinched, as if holding the remains up, over a cliff, of something which had long fallen sharply at the indent of her cheekbones.

César didn't know what to say. He stared at her. There was an eye, curved like a drying leaf. There was the nose, sloping towards her mouth. The mouth. Lips crisscrossed with minuscule lines, like baked bread. *Her mouth must be very dry*, he thought. As he took in her whole face, he saw that there was something very odd about it. He couldn't say she was deformed, nor even unattractive, but her features gave the troubling feeling that something was not in its proper place.

The woman held César's gaze, waiting for an answer. Her stare was blunt. She seemed to be willing him to speak.

"Me...te...mo..." César started. *Me temo que lo iba a matar.*

"I'm afraid I was going to kill you," César said, though he could barely believe such words could come out of his mouth.

The woman pursed her lips together, then released them. *Demasiado tarde para eso ahora.* "Too late for that now," she said. *Es una pena, Julio César.* "Too bad, Julio César."

César's heart strained at the sound of his full name. The woman raised her long fingers and drew them through the dark fluidity of her hair. Not a single tangle.

"I go by César now. Just César."

The woman smiled heavily. "Very refined, very *European*...Please excuse me, *César*. As for me, I still have my old, *brutish* name: Rosa."

César's gut clenched.

"What happened to you...*Rosa*?"

Rosa looked deeply at César. Her eyes seemed to be giving off steam. She took his hand and guided his fingers through her hair as if they were slipping through water. César's fingertips felt wet. But then he realized it was his eyes which were wet. His tears fell through the years, and landed at the feet of a girl standing at the window, watching a car drive away.

2

There seemed to be no connection between the questions César was asking and the answers Rosa was giving. César wondered if she could hear him.

"After you left," Rosa began, "I moved north to another village to work as a receptionist at a small hotel. My manager, who was exactly my father's age, took notice of me. He gave me the best shifts, sneaked fresh cakes from the kitchen into my locker...part of me was terrified of him. He greased his hair back and shaved his face every day. We got married."

"Did you love him?" César asked.

"…He didn't ask me to sing for him. He didn't know I had a good voice. Did you know I had a good voice, César?"

César paused. "That's what they used to say…but I never heard it either…"

"Well…maybe you should have listened closer…" Rosa replied. "He didn't listen very closely either, *my man*. I was his young, ugly bride. For some, this is enough…We got married. After our wedding ceremony, we went to stay in the hotel suite, because he was the manager. He asked me if I wanted to take a bath, and ran the water for me carefully, making sure it wasn't too hot. He tested the temperature on his wrist, like for a baby. He told me to put my wedding dress back on. He told me to take my hair down. He told me to get into the tub.

"I picked one foot up and pierced the bathwater with my toe. I dropped one foot into the water. Then the other. I was standing in the tub and he was crouched near the edge, like a little boy. He dipped his right hand into the water, then drew it around my ankle, then moved it up my calf. He continued upwards, over the back of my knee. Then around my thigh. He let his fingertips slide beneath my underwear. The underwear was a coarse white lace. He hooked his fingers underneath the lace and pulled down. The underwear stuttered. He tugged again, but it wouldn't slide completely off. He brought his other hand up and pulled both sides down so that the underwear came off and floated in the bathwater around my ankles.

"He told me to pull the skirt of my wedding dress up higher so that he could see. I pulled it up to my waistband and held it there. He dipped his other hand into the warm water, cupping some, bringing it towards him and turning his cupped palm over his head. The water trickled down his temples. He closed his eyes as the water ran over his face. Then he must have opened them. He brought the hand back into the water, then drew it upward, inside my thigh.

"I couldn't see him anymore because I was holding the bulky white lace skirt at my waist, trying to keep it from falling. Suddenly his fingers were inside me. I almost fell into the tub. He caught me and laid me down. My skirt floated in the water, my white lace underwear around my ankles still, like a wet spider web. My black hair soaked into the water and wavered around my breasts. He stepped into the tub over me. I could see his erection bulging above me in his trousers. He lowered himself to his knees. The ends of his trousers got wet and stuck to his calves. My hands lifted out of the water and moved towards his body. I caught something falling from his chest. His gold chain with a cross on it. Droplets of water rolled down my arm and fell onto my cheek.

"He caught my hands and clasped them together, then folded them into my throat, right under my chin. My fingers were crumbled into each other, illegible. He pushed and pushed my balled-up hands into my own throat. My breath pulled in and was immediately pushed out. He pressed in with his full weight.

"My knees twitched up. My tongue began to flail inside my mouth. He squeezed all my breath out of me. "

3

"He never heard me sing. Like you. I left this world his young, ugly bride."

4

"The story was in the papers and on the television, you know. With a photo of me that my mother had picked out, a flattering photo actually—my mother always knew how to make the best of a bad situation. The light in the photo smoothed out my features. I looked tragically erotic like one of those American child stars. I think you would have liked this photo of me, *César...*

"…He was sent to prison, my one-day husband. Not because he took the life out of me. But because he did it in such a special way, you know. With my own hands. He was sent to a special prison for that. On those islands, in the archipelago off the coast of Nayarit: *Islas Marias,* named after the Three Marys in the Bible. On the main island, the Mother Maria Island, there's the Federal Penal Colony. No fences or gates or electric wires. The island is its own vigil. The inmates live in a version of freedom, one could say, no chains or locks. They walk around the chapped walkways with heavy footsteps beneath the oily sun. The guards have faces that resemble the inmates. One thing that separates them is the uniform. The criminals wear beige pants and shirts. To the left of their hearts is their inmate number, printed on their shirts. The guards wear dark pants and a white shirt. They have no printed number. The guards have names and guns."

She smiled briefly, then let her mouth close in like a wound. She trailed off for a bit and walked in silence. The air smelled of a peeled fruit, a ripe familiar smell he couldn't quite place. Rosa started nodding as she walked, perhaps to music in her head. Her eyes drifted closed, yet she continued walking, nodding gently, with her long black hair undulating behind her. She began to recite:

"*But Mary stood outside by the tomb weeping, and as she wept she stooped down and looked into the tomb. And she saw two angels in white sitting, one at the head and the other at the feet, where the body of Jesus had lain. Then they said to her, 'Woman, why are you weeping?' She said to them, 'Because they have taken away my Lord, and I do not know where they have laid Him.' Now when she had said this, she turned around and saw Jesus standing there…*"

Rosa opened her eyes and looked at César.

5

"You know what he found there, on that penal colony, *my man.*

He found the miracle of God. One afternoon, he ran up those sun-bleached steps with sand encrusted into his knees, saying that Jesus came to him. *My man*, he looked straight up at the sun, with a bit of drool coming from the chapped crease between his lips. He looked as far as he could look, because his eyes were free, the freest part of his body. His sight now was his soul, he looked to see if he could see behind the clouds, if his soul could penetrate the invisible barriers, if it could penetrate the clouds and stratosphere and slip into *the holy villa*. His mouth trembled for prayer. Recitations from his childhood dribbled out. His voice was coarse and flaked between a man's and a boy's. He clasped his hands together and pressed them into his chest, pounding and babbling into the sun.

"I was there, too, actually. Just visiting, you could say. I was standing with the hot sand cushioning my toes. He did not see me. I was far off behind him. But even if I was right in front of him, he wouldn't have seen me. Every now and then I had to remind myself of this. When you look at someone, it is very hard to believe that they may not be seeing you too…

"I walked toward the crouching man until I was within arm's reach. With each step towards him, I told myself, even if he turns his head now, even if he stands up and turns around, he will not see me. I raised my hand and hovered it over his thick shoulder, watching him rock and shake and drone in his prayer. My hand felt very strong. Could I crumble this man's whole head in it, like an unwanted letter? *My man.* I did not crumble his head. I placed my hand upon his shoulder and held it there. His body flinched then let go of the tremble. He became still and peaceful. He looked around himself, dumbfounded and asked with a shy voice: *Jésus…?*

"This was funny to me. I wanted to laugh. But as soon as my mouth began to smile, I felt very pained, very sad. I straightened my mouth and it went away. He looked about him slowly, attentive for a signal. The beach remained as it was. The clouds in the sky continued to roll. The sun pressed its thumb upon the land.

"'...*Jésus?*' He asked with more confidence. I kept my mouth very straight. He glanced around him, to the sea, to the sky, back inland. No response. I can see him exactly as he was in that moment. Although I was behind him, I could see every muscle of his face. His face was singed with pink from the sun. He looked like a baby pig with cataracts trying to see his mother.

"I took my hand that was on his shoulder and smoothed it across towards his spine. At his spine, I spread my fingers and lightly drew them across the back of his neck, towards his hairline. At the first touch, he jolted his neck to the side. Then to the other.

"'*Jésus!*' I grazed the back of his neck again with my fingertips and he flinched his head once more and yelped, 'Jésus?!' He was laughing now. He was crying. He fell forward and caught himself with his palms in the sand, then lifted himself up and wiped the tears from his face, covered his skin like sandpaper.

"'*Perdóname. Sálvame. Bendice a mí.* 'Forgive me. Save me. Bless me.' He kept repeating for lack of prayer. Those were the only words he could pull together in time, the only words that felt clean enough.

Perdóname. Sálvame. Bendice a mí.
Perdóname. Sálvame. Bendice a mí.
Perdóname. Sálvame. Bendice a mí.

"The more he repeated, the more tightly I grasped his neck and massaged it, around the sides and up the spine and into the back of his skull, through the buzzed hair, and down his vertebrae. His knees were pinned into the sand, but his head was turning loosely around and around like in a trance.

"I took my hand off and he fell mouth-first into the sand. His hands remained limp at his sides. He exhaled into the sand and some of it tunnelled up his nose. He spoke into the grains. *He sido bend-ecido por tu amor.* 'I am blessed by your love.'

"I realized that there was a tear rolling down my cheek. It was small and oily and filled with pain. I leaned down over him. The tear rolled heavily down and dropped straight into that worm-skinned ear of his.

"*Vete a la chingada.* 'Go fuck yourself,' I whispered.

"He smiled so big and blessed with his mouth wide open, so the sand mixed in with his saliva and gullied down his throat."

6

Rosa stopped walking. She turned away from César and put her face into her hands. It was not a gesture of sadness. It was more like suddenly her face became too heavy and would fall off unless she held it in place.

"Rosa," César touched her shoulder. "Are you all right?"

"The worst is to lose your gratitude for life. To no longer see the grace in the living..."

He wished he had the words to console her, to lessen her pain, to ease her memories. But before he could think of something else to say, he heard a familiar melody. His body leaned in. Rosa was singing.

Gracias a la vida...

que me ha dado tanto...

Her voice was like nothing he had ever heard before. It seemed to be coming from miles away, lacquered and greasy. He felt it coursing through him like his own blood.

Me dio dos luceros, que cuando los abro,

Perfecto distingo lo negro del blanco

As she sang, she lowered her hands and turned towards César. Her hair was much thinner now, flat, parted straight in the center. Her cheeks were rounded, her mouth wider, curved downward, and her eyes closer together.

7

César watched Rosa's face changing. Her features were becoming someone else's, and he recognized them immediately. His chest swelled with awe and his eyes grew tender.

"*Violeta Parra…*" he said, enamoured.

The woman smiled at him and continued to sing. César picked up, mouthing along with her words. He trailed Violeta's voice like a child stumbling to keep up with the grown-ups.

As his voice stumbled on, he noticed an odd sound, underneath their singing, like a strange woodwind. His voice faded and it was just Violeta Parra singing. Still, that odd sound persisted, light, sweeping like dust underneath her voice.

A wind blew, and the half-breath whistle rose beneath her voice. Her eyes deepened like two cotton balls soaked in ink.

She was turning her head away from César. As she turned, César saw it. The bullet hole in the side of Violeta Parra's head. It tunneled precisely through from one side to the other. A gust of wind blew through the hole. Flute music came out of her head.

8

Violeta raised her hands and placed them over the holes in her head. Her wrists turned towards each other and covered her eyes. When she took her hands away, it was Rosa's face looking at César.

"You'll carry a bit of my pain, won't you, *César*?" Rosa said. "If you carry it long enough, it'll become your own."

She leaned into him and placed her lips upon his temple. She whispered each syllable into the flesh of his scalp, into the bone of his skull: *Pres-ta-das cos-as nos po-seen.* "Borrowed things possess us."

Then, she turned around and began to walk away. "Rosa!" César tried to call out, but the name did not leave his mouth. It curled on his tongue like a leaf-worm. Now, as she was leaving, she was frightening him. "ROSA!" he tried again, but nothing sounded. Just when he felt his heart would burst, a voice came close to César and fogged his ear like a whisper.

"I'll email you," Rosa said.

9

The marble twilight of the sky faded into a blue-gray of early evening. Lights in the windows. Voices in the buildings. This street was inhabited. The city was alive.

From far off, in the horizon, a black dot continued to breathe. It breathed with the breath of the people in the city of Paris, and the people of other cities too. It breathed with the breath of a girl far away, stepping into a car one leg at a time. And the breath of the actor on the TV screen. And the breath of the singer in the spotlight. And the breath of those who breathe and breathe and still can't remember who they are.

VII

YOUNG WOMAN, IN WINDOW, FROM THE WAIST UP, HAIR UNDONE AND BRUSHED

1

BÉATRICE IS FLAT-CHESTED, TEN years old, blonde as the sand. The seawater drools on to the shore. The sky is erased, ragged with clouds. They've rented a house, her father and the good friend he's kept from childhood, Marcel. Marcel has brought his family.

Marcel's daughter, Sabine, has her hair in two thick chestnut braids. She likes to go scavenging and give names. "Glinglink," she says and points at a cap from a beer bottle poking out of the sand. After that, every time anyone sees a bottle cap, they must pronounce it "glinglink." Emmanuelle plays in the sand joyfully with her mother. Béatrice is told to play with the girl who insists that the world must be named, though she would rather bury her toes in the sand one by one.

The girl takes her hand and they run off together. When they've reached the top of the beach, she lets go and runs far ahead. Béatrice calls out her name so she'll wait for her. The girl abruptly stops her sprint, turns around and runs straight back to Béatrice. The girl grabs her wrist and looks her straight into the eyes.

"I didn't give you permission to say my name."

Béatrice tries to excuse herself, but it's already too late, as the girl's hand is pinching her jaw open. The girl shoves two fingers in Béatrice's mouth and pushes into her jaw hinge so she can't bite her.

The girl's fingers go deep, and Béatrice gags immediately and twists in every way she can.

"Next time you say it without permission, you'll have to throw up your lunch."

The girl pulls her fingers out and lets go. Béatrice wipes off her mouth. She turns to look back at the shore where her mother is playing with her sister. She sees Marcel open a new beer bottle and hand it to her father. As the father takes it, he catches the figure of his daughter in the distance looking at him. He lifts the bottle high and shouts, "Haaaving fuuuunn, aaaannnggggeeelll...?"

Béatrice nods, not sure if she is nodding to her father or to the girl's newly set rule. The girl takes Béatrice's hand into hers.

"Come on, *angel*," she says.

Béatrice is now careful not to call the girl *Sabine*. The girl leads her through the dunes, away from their parents. She tells her which rocks to pick up. She tells her snail shells are where people hide their diamonds. She tells her to hurry up. Béatrice feels her white shoulders burning up and tells the girl that they are starting to sting. The girl replies that everyone's made of fire and whenever we get angry, pieces of ourselves spark off. That's what stars are, she explains, crumbs of our anger.

The girl has Béatrice examine the rocks they've collected because she left her glasses with her mom so they wouldn't fall off and break. After they've collected enough rocks, the girl finds a dry tree over the hump of a dune and sits down in its shade. Béatrice stands idle until the girl tells her to come and sit down. Béatrice sits, facing the girl.

The girl speaks in a factual tone, and Béatrice is afraid to contradict her. Together, they crouch and place the rocks in a circle formation between them, piling them as high as the middle of their thighs. "This is a portal," the girl explains. "Now we can see the future."

The girl bends her body over the rock circle, until the tip of her nose is directly facing the sand. "Hold my feet so I don't fall in," she tells Béatrice. Béatrice comes around behind the girl, crouches back down and takes hold of the girl's ankles.

"What do you…see…?" Béatrice asks timidly.

"Ha! I see YOUR future!" the girl responds.

Béatrice flinches. She regrets asking the question. She wants nothing to do with her future. Béatrice suddenly has the sharp sensation that knowing any part of your future is knowing how you will die. Her bottom lip coils under. *Please, please don't tell me how I die.*

"WELL, YOU WANNA KNOW WHAT I SEE?" the girl yells into the sand, as if her voice has to carry far, now that she is inside Béatrice's future, years away. Béatrice tries to push the sound out, the sound that will tell the girl to close the portal. She pushes from her toes up, but her throat is dry.

"HELLO, CAN YOU HEAR ME?" the girl shouts again into the sand.

Béatrice tries again. She must tell the girl to get out of her future. She pushes, but only the sound of a leaf shaking comes from her mouth.

"OH, YOU WON'T BELIEVE WHAT I'M SEEING! READY TO KNOW YOUR FUTURE?"

Béatrice grips the girl's ankles as if to signal her to stop. *Please, please, please.* But already a different voice is on its way. An inhale deepens her eyes and rises to the surface, like a metal gate lifting from a bull's cage. The voice comes. It is not a child's voice. It's a woman's voice. Béatrice's voice, twenty-some years later.

"Tell me," the voice speaks from Béatrice's mouth.

Béatrice's hands go limp and let go of the girl's ankles. The girl falls into the future, blood from her nose stains the sand, now, then.

On the shore, near their parents, the ocean water coils and rolls forward. For years to come, the waves wash the girl's scream away.

2

Béatrice stood wearing the long, black lace dress, her hand on the green curtain, opening an eyehole into the boutique. She peered out towards the shopkeeper who had just welcomed a woman named *Polina*.

The woman in question had her back to Béatrice. Her beige trench coat hung to her calves. Her brown hair curled over her shoulders. Her hands were leisurely resting in her coat pockets. Behind her, through the window onto the street, rows of bodies walked in both directions. Their mouths were moving, but made no perceptible sound. The only noise in the shop was the static coming from the radio. Then, the singer's voice emerged. "*Vida.*" the woman sang again. This time like a question. The strum of the guitar rose just then and seemed to calm the singer's question. Béatrice pulled the curtain a little wider and two wooden rings clacked into each other. The shopkeeper turned her head. The tips of her black hair scraped the paper of the open notebook on the desk. The woman in question took her hands out of her pockets and turned towards Béatrice as well. Their eyes met.

"Now, then," Polina said, "let's see the dress."

3

The singer's voice from the radio was fading away and only the guitar played her footsteps, leaving the song. Then the white walls were once again filled with the sound of dry hands rubbing together.

Béatrice stood in the boutique light, right in front of the open curtain. The skin of the black lizard dress was tightly wrapped around her body, stark against her blonde chignon and her mauve lips.

The green curtain behind her was gathered to one side and hung like a sheet of moss. Polina stood in the middle of the room, her hands in her coat pockets, observing Béatrice's body. The shopkeeper turned to face Béatrice.

Béatrice was held in place by their gaze. She felt herself leaning from the eyes of one woman to the eyes of the other.

She was not sure where to look. She wanted to observe Polina, to take the time to study her face, but as she traced her shoulder, up her neck, around her chin and to the hairline behind her ear, she felt her eyes were being repelled from seeing her face.

Béatrice's eyes drifted from Polina's body on to the street behind her, outside the glass window of the shop. She saw a pigeon-faced man veering towards the window. He shuffled forward so eagerly that he almost ran his nose into the glass. He pulled his chin back and adjusted his head to a secure distance from the glass. Since it was difficult to estimate exactly where this invisible surface was, his head bobbed like a slow-boiling potato.

Behind the man, a teenage boy came forward. One side of his mouth was stretching up as his eyes protruded, glossy like saliva from a kiss. He was staring. Then he cut his face to the side and let out a bark. He brought his arm out and wound his hand toward himself, until his two friends came to join. There they stood, the boiling potato, the saliva-eyes and his two chicken-legged friends in their bunched-up jeans, all staring at Béatrice.

She felt her skin tighten beneath the lace. She was cold. Goosebumps pushed towards the surface. Béatrice looked down at her breasts. They were abundant, white, held up by a thick, black satin bra. Beneath them her white stomach, then her underwear, black lace as well. She felt her pubic hair reaching between the thinly woven black strings. She looked down. There were her legs and her bare knees.

She had nothing on beneath the long black lace dress except for her structured bra and her transparent underwear. Béatrice wanted to snap her arms over her body and run behind the curtain, but the women's eyes would not let her move. The potato man's mouth was hanging open. Behind him, a woman walking past stopped and darted her eyes at Béatrice. Her mouth was sour, as if preparing to say the word "unfortunate." She quickly looked away and walked off.

One of the boys tapped on the glass of the window with his knuckles and said something that made another boy lick his puffy bottom lip. The third boy pushed his tongue into the side of his cheek repeatedly.

It was unbearable to be on display like this, fastened in place by the women's gaze. Béatrice grew lightheaded, as if she were stretching away from herself. Just then, Polina turned sharply towards the boys behind the window. They stumbled into each other, then scattered. Béatrice's forearms sprang closed over her breasts and she ran back behind the green curtain.

The older man continued standing there, his mouth open, bobbing to the memory of Béatrice's breasts.

4

Béatrice stood alert behind the curtain, her arms still wrapped over her chest.

She heard the women continue talking uneventfully, sometimes one of their heels took a step this way or that, but neither came back to see her.

Good. Stay away.

Her teeth clenched down and sucked in the flesh of her cheeks. A taste accumulated in her throat, bitter as grapefruit, thick as yogurt. She thought of the shopkeeper's bare forearms lain apathetically upon the starched pages of the open notebook as she looked Béatrice up and down. She thought of the woman named *Polina* and her black-magnet face that repelled the eyes from seeing. Those boys behind the window staring at her, those boys and their easy adolescence. Yes, it must be *easy*, Béatrice thought. And the old man and his open mouth and his breath like a fly's wings rubbing together. His eyes on Béatrice, assuming a right to her body. The memory rippled through her like nausea.

A set of fingers slid around the curtain's edge and began to pull. The shopkeeper walked in, past Béatrice as if she were not there, to the table with the sewing machine. She pulled off the woolen shawl and swung it around her shoulders. She paused then, and looked at the metal needle of the sewing machine.

"Well, have you decided about the dress?" she said as if to the needle.

5

The woman named Polina came into the doorway, the beginnings of a smile playing across her burgundy-painted lips.

Béatrice's gaze drew upwards over the small valley below her nose where the skin stretched into a smile. Over each wide eye, the dark stroke of an eyebrow. Her hair was much lighter, an almond color. It fell generously to the left.

Béatrice began hesitantly. "How...much is it?" she asked.

Polina's eyes glimmered like shards from broken bottles.

"How much is the dress. How much is the dress..." the shopkeeper echoed to herself.

Béatrice waited. Polina relaxed her lips and took a long breath in.

"...You know sometimes people pay more for a dress than..." she finally said.

Béatrice waited. The shopkeeper was already gone and the heavy green curtain was swaying.

6

"The dress is on me," Polina said. She walked over to the stacked chair, took it off the boxes and set it on its feet beside Béatrice. "Take a seat."

Béatrice did not know if she should sit here with this woman. But her spine made contact with the wooden back of the chair and she knew she had accepted.

"You are very rigid, don't be so rigid."

"Okay," Béatrice said.

"You wanted a dress, you got one."

Béatrice stayed silent.

"Don't you like the dress?"

"Yes."

"Good. There's no reason you shouldn't. You've got a very beautiful body, are you aware of this? Of course you are aware. I won't make you go through the banality of the beginning of this conversation. Your breasts are especially nice."

"I know," Béatrice said like a sullen child.

"Well then. Why are you so unhappy?"

"Who says I'm unhappy," Béatrice said. Her arms locked across her gut.

"No one. Are you happy?"

"No, I'm not."

"Good. I value sincerity. I am being sincere with you, I hope you know. Now, if you're satisfied with your body, why aren't you happy?"

"I don't care about my body."

"Maybe you don't, but others seem to. Don't you care about them?"

"If they care about my body, I don't care about them."

Béatrice was now in sync with Polina. She was ready to strike back. Polina raised her hand towards Béatrice's face. With the tips of her fingers, Polina dabbed Béatrice's temple, then slid her fingers up Béatrice's chignon.

"I don't care about your body, *Béatrice*."

The way Polina said her name pulled Béatrice open like a tin can. Her mind was full of questions that squirmed against each other.

"There are people who leave their bodies and their bodies go on living without them," Polina said. "These people are named Natasha."

7

"Na...ta...sha..." Béatrice repeated unconsciously under her breath. She heard the individual sounds, but could not hear the name they were meant to form.

"*Telo...Nomer...Chiffre...Youpka...*" Polina said very quietly as if counting.

Béatrice's eyes grew thin, trying to listen.

"*Anja...Sofia...Salomeya...Viktoria...*" Polina continued her count.

VIII

TO MOSCOW!

1

CÉSAR STOOD MOTIONLESS IN the street where the woman who was at once Rosa and Violeta had left him. A persistent buzz rummaged in his pocket. He pulled out the object and held it in his palm. It was his cell phone, ringing. He read the name of the caller out loud, "Marcel." His agent was calling.

2

The last time his agent called him was a month ago. César had grabbed the phone eagerly, ready to run to an audition. But Marcel was just calling to check that the height listed on his CV was still *good-to-go*. The time before that, he needed César to come by and re-sign some papers on which he had accidentally spilled coffee. Once he even called César on New Year's Eve. César had been handing a glass of cheap champagne to a new friend he had made at a party, José, when his phone rang. He pounced, dropping the glass, ready for some groundbreaking news regarding his acting career. If his agent was calling on such a day and at such an hour, it had to be important. But it turned out that all Marcel wanted to know was whether César still had all his teeth. When César confirmed that he did, the agent was disappointed. "Oh, just got word of a spot, they need a young Hispanic with missing teeth."

"Can't they just use a makeup artist for that?"

"Nah, they said they'd rather just get a kid with a couple of his teeth missing than pay one of those expensive makeup people hourly."

"Oh."

"That's how it goes. Anyways, keep me posted."

"Posted for what?"

"I mean if you happen to lose any teeth. Needa get back to them by Tuesday."

César spent that whole night paranoid he was going to crack a tooth on something. On the one hand, it would qualify him for this gig—whatever it was. On the other hand, teeth were expensive to get fixed, and the money he'd get from this job would most likely not cover repairing his teeth. Unless, of course, it was a well-produced feature film. And his character, a Hispanic with missing teeth, was a lead or at least a supporting character. Then again, what were the chances that there was a feature film being made about a young Hispanic man with missing teeth? Unless it was a sort of biopic story of some revolutionary Hispanic political figure. (Those were really taking off nowadays). César scanned his historical knowledge for any Hispanic politicians he could remember that had missing teeth in their young adult life.

The more he tried to think of historical toothless Hispanics, the more his heart began to race. *This was big*, he thought. *You idiot!* He had to get hold of his agent. César locked himself in the bathroom and called his agent repeatedly, but the phone kept ringing and ringing into the void. By the time everyone in the main room was yelling *Happy New Year* at each other and chugging their cheap champagne, César sat on his toilet seat, convinced he had ruined his life.

A couple of days later, he'd finally got hold of his agent only to find out that what had grown into a Spielberg biopic of Che

Guevara in his head was actually just a walk-on role in a drug-bust scene in a web series.

3

So this time, as his cell phone rang, César tried to contain his excitement.

"Hello. Hello, César. You hear me? It's Marcel."

"Yes, yes—"

"César, it's Marcel, your agent. You hear me okay over there. Where are you?"

"Yes, yes I hear you. I'm on the street, do you hear me?"

"Yes, I hear you. César, listen, I've got some pretty good news."

Steady, gecko, César told himself. But "good news" bounced around his chest like a racquetball.

"Yes?"

"Yes, oh yes, César! Some good news. You hear me over there?"

"Yes, I hear you. You don't hear me?"

"No, I hear you. Listen, César. Hope you are ready for this. This is the type of thing that could change a lot for you."

"Yeah?"

"You better believe it! What I'm telling you, César, is this: you gotta be a fisherman in this industry."

"Okay."

"You gotta get up early and dip your bait in that sea of opportunities and wait."

"Yeah."

"If you're a good fisherman, César, if you've got the patience, something'll bite. Now when it bites, then you can't be lazy-eyed with one foot asleep. You hear me over there, César?"

"Yeah, yes I do."

"You gotta flex and you gotta pull, César. You gotta reel that fish in. Big or small, sardine or shark, REEL IT IN."

César wondered if Marcel had ever really gone fishing.

"You ready to reel, César?"

"Yeah—yes, I'm ready."

"Good, good, 'cause that's exactly what you're gonna have to do *right now*. Hope your foot's not asleep, because, César, you got a *big fish* on your line."

"…Really?"

"I'm talking thirteen consecutive episodes on one of the most-watched TV series in France. You feel that fish, César?"

"Thirteen episodes?"

"Feel that fish pulling on your line?"

"Yea—s, I guess, but—"

"And let me tell you, thirteen episodes in *this* season, and the character doesn't die in the thirteenth, so in all logic, he's back in the next season. And maybe the next. And let me tell you something else: one of the producers just happens to be a good friend, so let's just say he values my eye when it comes to casting. You feel that fish now, César?"

"Yea—Yes, I mean—"

"Tell me you feel that fish, César."

"I…feel that fish."

"Can't hear you, not sure where you are, but shake out that foot, César, and tell Marcel you *feel* that *FISH* on your line."

"I…feel that fish on my line!" César yelped into the phone, wiggling the toes of his right foot.

"Good! Now, can you come by the office?"

The office is what Marcel called a room in his apartment with a chair on either side of a desk.

"Sure. Yes! Now?"

"Now, yes, of course, now. REEL IT IN." Then Marcel hung up.

4

César looked around. He didn't know where he was. A couple of parked motorcycles, two crooked trees. Rosa. Violeta. No one. Just the stone wall of a dead end.

From the dead end wall, a stone basin protruded, tiled with small bricks. This was the bottom of the small fountain—once. Now it was filled with half-wilted greenery, growing out from the loose pile of dirt at the bottom.

César remembered a girl he had met when he first moved to Paris. She was in the same international acting school as him. She spoke even less French than he did at the time, so they communicated in their broken English. She had deeply set eyes that held onto a shadow of sleep, and cheekbones that made him think of Yugoslavia. She was not from Yugoslavia, as it no longer existed, but she did have a heavy accent from elsewhere, Balkan maybe.

He liked listening to her speak. She drew out her syllables like a careful ballpoint pen. She gestured throughout her speech as if continually tying and untying a scarf. One day she mentioned her grandfather. He had died. She had to leave for the funeral. He had to be buried in the Jewish tradition.

"And what's that like?" César had asked.

"How I no? Zay get like a rabbi and he say like a Jewiss prayur maybe."

When César met her eyes, he saw there were a couple of thin red veins threading towards the pupil. He would have liked to reach out and put his hand on her shoulder.

"Zay call us Jewess like vi no what is dis, but no one no what is Jewes. Vi put togehzer what-is-means-*Jewiss* like internet-blog-forum and vi pretend to be Jewes togezur."

She explained that her grandfather's name was Mendel, and his mother's name was Golda, and even if they had never celebrated a Shabbat in their lives, such names must be buried by a rabbi.

As she continued to speak, César could feel a tightness in her words, as if what she was trying to express was balling up progressively and tangling into an inseparable knot. His hand grew heavier, unable to rise and comfort the girl.

"When are you coming back?" he finally asked.

The girl blinked then looked away. Her eyes drifted to the wall behind her. In a low voice, she spoke more to that open space than to César.

"I wish all grampas and gramas go into earth already and let me live new life…"

César wanted so deeply to say something in return that would make her previous statement a joke. He thought about nudging her lightly on the forearm and saying, "Let's kill 'em all then!" But as he rolled his tongue on the top of his mouth, the words couldn't find their beginning.

"I vant be great-time actriss, César…" the girl said with such desperation, César almost bit his own tongue by accident.

"…like on big international film…speaking French and speaking English! Here dis is…possible… Back…you know…" Her finger rose from her lap and pointed limply east, "there, not possible…"

She lowered her finger back down to the others. "Vy I have go back and be…not possible…?"

The girl sat still for a moment then suddenly looked sharply at César. "I am *so sad*, César, *so sad*, becuz I sink I can be *GREAT-IMPORTANT* for *HISTORIE!*"

She fixed her charged eyes on César, and looked to him as if she were being electrocuted. César held his breath and stared back. Finally, she let her shoulders go and looked down.

"…Ven I go back…" her finger rose again, pointing sleepily east, "ven I zere…I like…forget all dis. I sink only: you werth nahsing, stupitt gurl. Before werth nahsing, now werth nahsing, forward go werthing nahsing, forever stupitt gurl…"

After she left, César went online and looked up Jewish burial traditions. As he read from his computer screen, he imagined Mendel X'vich folded in his coffin. The coffin being lowered into the earth, and the rabbi pronouncing, *Al mekomo yavo veshalom.* "May he go to his place in peace."

Then, one by one, the family members would pierce the point of a shovel into the ground, lever a bit of soil and throw it into the grave. He heard precisely what the soil would sound like when it hit the wood of the coffin, like a set of pens suddenly dropped to the floor.

Months later, he received an email from her in an oddly jovial tone, not resembling the heavy voice she had left him with.

"You no, the grave-hole look like hole where big tooth pulled out. So, when I was stand at funeral, I was think this: Look at me, I stand inside big, big mouth where all time around me God pull teeth. Dis time he pull Grampa out. Ven he pull me?"

César had replied asking again when she'd be coming back to school. She never answered. She never came back to school. César convinced himself that she must be an established actress now at some national Balkan theater, playing roles like one of Chekhov's three sisters. The one who keeps hassling about Moscow. *To Moscow! To Moscow!* It was Irina's line, if memory served César correctly. Yes, Irina. The girl's name, though, he suddenly couldn't recall.

5

César scanned the old fountain as if searching for her name there. Above the rim of the basin, there was a stonework Egyptian head. Its eyes were hollow and its mouth was open, where a stream of water should have been.

Oddly enough, this small, unused fountain of weeds with its Egyptian head reminded César that he was in Paris. Paris, a city organized like a war survivor who keeps tucking his vestiges into nooks that have a sense of logic only to him. In passing, if the old fountain could speak, it would comment with a beady voice: "Oh yes, and this is from when I got liberated in Cairo and had to hitch-hike past those damn pyramids all the way home to your Gramma!"

César turned away from the dead end and walked toward the other end of the street. He looked at the street sign, *rue Alfred Stevens*. It opened onto another street, wider and populated with footsteps and passing cars. Without looking at that street name, César turned onto it and began to run. *Rue des Martyrs*.

IX

TELO, NOMER, CHIFFRE, YOUPKA...

1

POLINA CONTINUED TO SPEAK with an easy rhythm, her eyes surveying different parts of Béatrice's face.

Telo, Nomer, Chiffre, Youpka...

"...A woman from Eastern Europe can be sold for 800 US Dollars to, say, Amsterdam or Prague or Istanbul. Whether she's Bulgarian or Ukrainian or Latvian, to the customers, she's Russian. Whether she is Pavla or Olena or Salomeya, to the customers, her name is *Natasha*. Once the money is exchanged and her passport taken from her, it is then that she leaves her body."

2

"To go missing. What a phrase. Do you realize? As if *missing* is a place one must *get to*. One day someone leaves their house, goes for a walk, and walks and walks and walks, until they *get* missing."

3

Béatrice listened. The words floated out of Polina's mouth and seeped into Béatrice like clouds. Polina swept her hair behind her shoulder. She continued.

"I met an American woman who was traveling around the Ukrainian-Russian border, from Kharkiv to Belgorod, trying to trace her roots. You know the type, watercolor eyes, dusty hair cut into a bob, neat and efficient travel clothes and a pearly row of teeth inside her systematic smile. One of those *left-over-vich* generations. Dedicated. Even managed to learn a good basis of Russian and a couple of Ukrainian phrases. Then, at the Zheleznodorozhny train station in Belgorod, she had her wallet stolen. She ran up to a man who was looking at the timetable and panted in broken Russian that someone had stolen her wallet. The man scratched his coarse chin and followed the zipper down the center of her fleece jacket. He then pointed to the police office at the bottom of the escalator. She thanked the man excessively and hurried down the escalator. At the bottom, almost hidden from the foot circulation of the travelers was a closed door with *Politsiya* written on it. She tried the door, but it was locked. She looked at her watch (*At least I still have my watch*, she tried to remain positive). It was lunchtime. The police had to eat, she reasoned.

"The woman paced back and forth outside the door, only a few steps at a time. She thought of all the things in her wallet. She thought of their order and value. The small pieces of paper with new-found Russian words she had been collecting and trying to learn during her trip. The address of the American Embassy she had noted just in case. The photo of her ex-husband with his arm around their now-adult son. And, oh yes, which credit cards needed to be canceled in what order.

"Time passed, and the torn-off paper pieces, her ex-husband's arm around their son, the to-be-canceled credit cards, balled together until she felt bloated with a general sense of loss. She stopped pacing. Her hands drifted, touching the wall, the doorknob, the latched zipper of her fleece jacket. She smoothed her fingers around her the bone of her wrist, then came against the contour of her watch. She looked at it again. It may be time for tea now, she thought. The police here may drink their tea at this hour…

"She let her wrist go loose and time fell away. Her eyes wandered the walls. They traced the door frame, then followed across the floor line, then moved back up to a poster full of times in columns. She looked over lists of times, passing full days and starting over again, then her eyes drifted to a bulletin board next to the door of the police room. It was tacked with photocopies of faces and handwritten notes."

"Propavshi'yi bez vecti"

4

"In Russian, you don't have *to go* missing, it's a single verb. The verb sits next to your name and you're gone.

"In English you have to work for it. To go. Missing. You have to get up and walk there."

Polina leaned forward, closer to Béatrice.

"But you French are, as always, the most romantic. *Porté disparu.* The person must be carried forth missing. In France, there are lines of people waiting, with their arms out, bent elbows, hands cupped towards themselves, each holding a disappearance."

5

"Propavshi'yi bez vecti"
Missing without news

In Russia, in order to truly disappear, you must disappear physically and narratively. Since this woman had indefinite time on her hands—the time that was not stolen from her—she glanced at the faces on the board of Missing Persons, one by one.

One looked like a school photo of a girl, maybe thirteen, her hair was wooden-brown and cut jaggedly in layers above her shoulders. The aqua blue shirt she was wearing matched her aqua blue irises, which seemed to be standing back, shy, against the wall of her white pupils. She smiled, as if embarrassed to be there, to be photographed present. (Now that she was absent, she wouldn't have to be so embarrassed.)

Another was of a seventeen-year-old boy, slightly younger than her own son, with a bristled head, wide eyebrows around his two metal eyes. The photocopy was in black and white and used, so it was hard to tell when it was posted. Years, it must be. Now he may be old enough to be the father of the boy in the photo. She thought about this. She pictured both the father this boy should be now and the boy at the age of his disappearance standing the way her ex-husband and her own son stood in the photo that she had kept in her wallet. The father with his arm around his boy, holding onto each other's vanishing.

Then there was a man. Maybe thirty-three. He was in a living room, which looked like it was decorated for a film taking place in the '70s. This American woman looked over the patterns with her own nostalgia, then came back to the man. He had his shoulders turned away from the camera, but his neck facing the lens, as if surprised by the snapshot. He had a funny smile on his face, a mouthwatering joy. The woman almost smiled with the man instinctively. Maybe there was a birthday cake waiting in the next room for him. She read the text below. *Igor...*It was his wife that posted the note. *Last seen...waiting for bus...on...—skaya street...*Why would she choose such a happy picture of him? It made it seem like he enjoyed surprises and maybe even had a good laugh when he was so suddenly abducted.

The woman moved on to another note. She read the Cyrillic slowly, sliding her finger across the letters to help her move the sound along in her mind. She had to use her full concentration to sound out the words and understand them. *Irina...nine years old... left grandmother's house to buy milk...never returned...contact...* Irina had a round, fresh face, as if she had come in from playing in the snow. The American woman crouched down to see eye to eye with the girl. Her finger touched the girl's rosy cheek on the shiny photo, and it suddenly felt spongy and cool like a child's skin in wintertime. The girl's eyes were soft and trusting. The woman leaned in closer and looked into them.

The sound of keys clinked against each other. A police officer was unlocking the door. But the American woman did not move, her face fixed on the photo.

The officer wiggled the key out of the lock and turned the doorknob. He held the door open and looked at the woman. He said something to her in Russian that she did not hear or did not understand or maybe the police officer didn't say anything at all and it was the little girl who was speaking Russian to the woman.

Eto ya.

The policeman looked closer at the woman.

"*Eto ya.*" The woman repeated. Or maybe it was the little girl who said it.

Ya cibya nashla. "That's me. I found myself."

The woman pronounced it so finely and fluidly that it confused the policeman. By the looks of her, she was no doubt from the west, and yet the voice which came out of her was right at home.

He squinted and went into his office.

The woman pulled the photo off the bulletin board, folded it, and put it in her pocket. The little girl had been found. Then she walked out of the train station, found the nearest grocery store, and bought a bottle of milk.

She couldn't have proved much anyways, since she didn't have any ID, her wallet had been stolen. As it turns out, it's not that difficult to live without any ID in the Ukraine. Whenever anyone asked her her name, she'd reply, "*Natasha.*"

6

Telo, Nomer, Chiffre, Youpka… Polina repeated.

Telo

Body

Nomer

Number

Chiffre

Digit

Youpka

Skirt

Yulia

The name of her ten-year-old sister.

Pamyet

Memory

Stoyimact

Price

Imye, Name

Pizda, Cunt

Yvette, was her name

Istiyourum, I want

Attends ici, wait here

Hier zitten, sit here

Viktoria, was her name

Halt die Klappe, shut up

Irina, was her name

7

Young woman, in the window, from the waist up, hair undone and brushed.

Pogoulyim? a man's voice calls up. "Let's go for a walk," he proposes to the woman with no legs.

X

IS THAT YOUR FISH?

1

CÉSAR RAN, SIDE-STEPPING ALL obstacles, feet, stroller wheels, car bumpers. He had to get himself to Marcel's. He had no time to think about direction. He knew that if he just ran, his body would figure it out. His cheeks sponged up the cool air.

He ran down *rue Condorcet* then turned right on *rue de Rochechouart*. His ribs pulled him east, then veered him north until his feet slowed on a narrow street called *rue des Petits Hotels*.

He looked at the buildings on either side of him. The principal structure was a stone-faced middle school, *College Bernard Palissy*. After that, a pedicure boutique with hazed windows, closed for the weekend already. Then a couple of broad, disappointed-faced buildings which held *property* or *offices for sale* signs. Then again, this time to his right, another pedicure boutique, this one with its blinds drawn shut. Was this street inhabited by residents with feet in need of constant maintenance?

At the end of the street, on the corner, was a stationery and gift store, also closed. Through the windows, César could see packets of cards arranged geometrically, and pens and pencils packed into plastic containers. The paper selection was in a spectrum of pastel colors. Dim and peaceful, it looked like the newborn baby ward of a hospital, all those greetings waiting to be expressed.

César hadn't remarked on the name of the street when he turned onto it. If he had, he might have wondered why there wasn't a single hotel (little or big) on it. This, of course, would have lost him even more time.

His thoughts had already slowed his pace to an idle walk. *REEL IT IN, GECKO,* a voice sergeanted in his ear and whipped up the soles of his shoes. César took off once more in a sprint.

2

His feet were humid and the shirt beneath his zip-up was sticking to him. He was standing still on a busy street, panting, looking for a street sign.

An African woman walked towards him. Her violet dress was scattered with bright traces like orange peels. She had on a thick headscarf which was the same fabric, and knotted in bulk, on her forehead. Her breasts were pressed down by a piece of fabric with a different pattern, dark etchings, piles of grasshopper legs.

As she passed him, he noticed the baby wrapped upon her back with the scarf. The baby's cheeks spread like dough, eyes closed, as if he was listening to the creaking of his mother's spine. Just before crossing, a man came out of a fast-food shop wearing a long white cotton robe. The woman greeted him, her French words rolling in and out of another language.

César spotted it. *Rue du Faubourg St-Denis.* This was the street where Marcel lived. He hurried past an approaching couple to cross the street, but got intercepted by an Indian man holding a big bouquet of white and red roses. The man stopped straight in front of César and levered the bouquet into his face.

"No thanks," César quickly replied, trying to shoo the roses out of his nose. The Indian rose seller did not budge. César repeated *Non merci,* again, then again *Non merci.* Then someone turned around and bumped into the Indian man and like a pinball, he was set on his way, to offer roses elsewhere. Eager to cross, César lifted his foot, but it was pushed directly back down to the concrete. His toe was stubbed. *"Sorry, Pardohen,"* an American-looking girl said as she pulled her rolling suitcase after her. César got a glimpse of her face. She must have played the clarinet as a child and sided with her dad during the divorce.

Héy-O, César,
Ramène le poisson!

Marcel's voice bounced around in César's head. He looked back at the street, which was streaming with passing cars.

HÉ PUTA.

CARRETE dat FISH!

This voice was his brother Raul's, compact and gritty.

Then, in the elastic voice of his younger, fatter brother, Alonzo.

Puuuuta, carrete ese pez!

"Estoy tambaleando! I am!"

César... (Rosa's voice. It sounded disappointed in him.)

"I'm waiting for the cars to pass..."

César... (Rosa's voice was smoothing out now, as if freshly ironed.)

"Yeah?"

¿Es tu pez?

¿Qué?

Is that your fish, Julio César?

"Sí, si, esa es mi pez."

Dunt looz it, César. You get onlee wone...

"I won't."

Grampa got bahreed with hiz fish under hiz two crossid hands...

"¿Qué?"

Juan-Miguel the hothead was growing impatient.

REEL IT IN YOU PEESOV SHIT! he spouted.

"*I'm reeling I'm reeling!*" César exclaimed, opening his arms wide to the world.

His upper arm ran into something cushioned. He turned his head and searched for the source. It was a prostitute's large breast.

3

"Hello," the prostitute said ironically.

This big-breasted woman seemed at first glance old enough to be his mother. But when César looked closer, her eyes had dilated and her pupils were glossy like a mesmerized baby's. As soon as she blinked, though, her eyelids lifted back up, revealing the drooling vision of an elderly woman trying to remember.

César quickly pulled his elbow back towards his gut and excused himself. The woman lifted her finger, on which she was wearing a keyring. Off the metal ring was one big bronze-colored key which looked like it was meant for a castle. The apartment buildings in this city were so old that it was not uncommon to have such a key. Next to that long key, other smaller, more modern keys hung, perhaps for a mailbox or a storage space. She jingled the keys to show César that she had a room upstairs where she could take him (unlike some other prostitutes, who don't have a room of their own and have to use the street as their oyster).

"Uh, oh, no thanks," César said and stepped in closer to the street curb, eyeing the passing traffic for gaps. None of the spaces aligned enough to give César a pathway across. As he waited, he could hear the discreet metal clink of the keys hanging from the prostitute's finger behind him.

4

The light flashed red and the cars screeched to a halt in a bristled line. One motorcycle managed to slip through the congestion and peel off just before the crowd of pedestrians ebbed in. César stepped into the street with a crowd of others. He crossed with them, away from this prostitute who could have been his mother, or an infant, or an elderly woman with Alzheimer's… He heard her rattling keys following after him. He could feel her, standing somewhere behind him with an arched chest, jingling her keys, her body morphing between ages like a girl growing up in front of a funhouse mirror.

As he walked, the keys jingled in his ear on loop. They were beginning to sound like the voice of a man being fast-forwarded to repeated flashes of giddiness. César listened closer to the chirping, trying to decipher the words. With every step, it chirped again. And again. *Notereconoces? Notereconoces?*

No te reconoces?

Don't you recognize yourself? the jingling keys seemed to be saying to him.

XI
VERY NICE

1

BÉATRICE WENT HOME WITH the dress in a plastic bag.

Jean-Luc, her sister's boyfriend, was in the kitchen. He was standing with his back to her, holding the refrigerator door open. He closed the fridge and turned around with a plastic bottle of Perrier in his hand.

"Oh. Hello," he said to Béatrice and gave her a kiss on each cheek.

"Hello," she replied, and went into the living room.

Her mother was there, turning an oriental vase towards the light. Her father was on the sofa reading the paper. He lowered it and glinted at Béatrice.

"Whatchyou got in the bag?" her father asked.

"A dress," Béatrice replied.

Béatrice looked through the living room doorway to the flight of stairs that led up to the first floor. She longed to go upstairs with the dress and to be alone with Polina's voice, which was still floating around in her head. She wanted to feel the lace on her body and to look at herself in the mirror and think about the stories Polina had told her.

"Try it on," Emmanuelle said, from the top of the stairs. She was wearing tight jeans and a loose silk shirt which hugged the smooth cups of her bra beneath. As she bent forward, the silk shirt hung down and showed her breasts, which were pushed gently together like two hotel pillows.

"Yeah, honey, give us a show," her father added.

Béatrice turned. Her mouth was open and a voice was already leaving her.

"*Okay*," the voice said meekly.

It was quieter than Béatrice's voice, smaller because it was coming from far away. Years back. Twenty-some years back. From a sandy dune where her hands are holding a girl's ankles.

2

In her room, Béatrice rummaged in the drawers for something black to wear underneath the dress. She found a black tank top and skirt, and covered her body with the thin, tight cotton. She pulled the dress out of the bag and slid each arm in carefully, then pulled its length down. *Telo, Nomer…* She bent her arms back and pulled the zipper all the way up her spine. *Chiffre…*

She went to the small mirror above her dresser, only low enough to reflect her face. She could feel where her chignon had come undone. *Hier zitten.* She smoothed the loose strands of hair up, until they were all together and sleek like a highway at dawn.

She looked down. Her feet were bare. *Sofia.* She found the black heels she wore for concerts. They were highly arched, but with a strong base that she could use to tap the rhythm as she sang. She could feel the coarse black lace on her body. She stepped her foot into each heel slowly, as if into bathwater.

Imye. Yulia. Istiyourum.

3

Béatrice stood at the top of the stairs, with her father, mother, sister, and Jean-Luc all gathered together to look at her. From below, she was a wartime ghost or the mistress to a politician.

"Oh la la la!" the father said.

Jean-Luc inserted a *bravo* and let his chin nod.

Emmanuelle and her mother remained quiet, giving the first round of words to the men. The women took their time to listen and observe, using their silence strategically.

"Come on down, Marilyn!" the father burst out joyfully.

The mother glanced over at her husband's grin.

Béatrice lifted one side of the dress which parted at the slit, her white knee emerging from the partition. Emmanuelle looked at her boyfriend, then at her father, then back at Béatrice. She came up to Béatrice and stroked her forearm, feeling the ripples of lace.

"It's really—very—nice—the dress," Emmanuelle said, her fingertips running over the weave-work of the lace.

Her mother reached over, sliding a set of three fingers down the lace.

"Not too itchy?" the mother asked.

Béatrice shook her head. Jean-Luc reached out his hand hesitantly and touched the black lace on Béatrice's collarbone.

"It is—very nice," he pronounced.

Emmanuelle's eyes dropped straight to where Jean-Luc's fingertips were placed on her sister's collarbone. The father shot a look at Jean-Luc. Jean-Luc pulled back his hand and stepped closer to Emmanuelle. The father took a large step toward Béatrice and reached out his hand, confident, bold, as he too wanted to tell his daughter that the dress was very nice. He placed his hand on Béatrice's shoulder and squeezed it mildly.

"Very nice," he affirmed.

The mother glanced at the father. Emmanuelle glanced up at Jean-Luc. Jean-Luc tried to meet Emmanuelle's gaze. But as his eyes descended they tripped and fell onto Béatrice's throat. As soon as they realized where they were, they scrambled back, trying to correct the error, but stumbled again and landed straight on the father's back. Upon feeling the ocular attention of someone behind him, the father glanced back and spotted Jean-Luc. Jean-Luc quickly pulled his eyes back, hovering them vaguely in space, suspicious of their destination. The mother turned her head towards Emmanuelle. Emmanuelle now peered at her father, who was peering at Jean-Luc, whose eyes were swarming around Béatrice's feet, in search of discretion.

Emmanuelle looked up at Béatrice. Their mother looked at her husband. He did not see as he was watching Jean-Luc. Jean-Luc looked up at the ceiling, then down at an oriental rug in front of the couch, then finally at a glimmer of light shining off a ceramic vase on the coffee table.

Béatrice's eyes followed the movement of everyone else's eyes, jumping from one another like children playing in a minefield. Her sister moved into Jean-Luc and nudged her head onto his shoulder. Jean-Luc drew his eyes off Béatrice and put his arm around Emmanuelle, who in return said under her breath: *meow, meow.*

XII

MARCEL

1

OUTSIDE MARCEL'S BUILDING STOOD a tall, young black man, Nigerian maybe. He held a cell phone in his hand and was rolling his eyes from left to right, as if reading the street. César stepped into the doorway and the man peeled his back off the building wall and walked into the text of bodies he had just been reading.

2

On the right-hand side of the doorway was a flat steel-colored plate with rows of buttons, 1 to 9 and 0, and the options A and B. This was the building security system. No matter how shabby the residence or neighborhood, every building in Paris has one of these door codes. Type in the secret code, and *voilà* the door beeps or the lock clicks and just push to open. However, there is a more impressive option. Type in the code, beep, click, and just as you lift your hands to push the door open, it cuts away from its frame and opens all by itself before you. Automatic. To César, this was indeed quite impressive, so impressive that every time he visited Marcel he completely forgot that the world had advanced to this level of innovation and would raise his hands up and push in every time, nearly falling through the automatically opening door.

This time it was no different. César typed in the code and raised his hands to push just as the door clicked and moved open. He grabbed the side of the door frame and his elbow scraped against the wall's side as he tripped his way inside. He heard someone calling out to him and turned, seeing the Nigerian man across the street pointing at him and saying something like *Kana a'ya ka fito*. César liked the way it sounded. Kana-aiye-ka-fee-too, he almost wanted to call back in solidarity. But then the automatic door hit him on the side of his head as it closed.

.

3

César hit the button for Marcel's apartment. After a moment, the door to the stairway buzzed. His excitement began to rise, and his legs found their bounce. He hopped up the first stairway, up the red-velvet slap of carpeting that was matted down over the stairs. One floor, turn up, another floor, turn up, he skipped up the stairs with long strides. On the fourth floor, he took a right and went down the hallway, passing a door with a scratched-up lock. Marcel had told César that someone had broken into his neighbor's place in early August and, in Marcel's words, "picked the crumbs off the floor." This made César imagine the burglars as a line of organized ants.

Marcel's door was the one next to it. No one had broken into his apartment in the twelve years he had lived there, Marcel made it known proudly. His door was painted a deep forest green. Towards the top was a small metal ring holding what seemed to be a glass marble. This was the eyehole. Just below the eyehole, etched into the wood, was an *X*, scratched in two crossing slivers of light brown wood. Below this *X* was another, similar in shape and size, also etched in with a blade of some sort. Below that *X* was another. And another. The *X*s descended in a totem line down Marcel's door, with the last *X* just above César's knee.

4

Marcel was not religious, nor spiritual, nor particularly sensitive to nature or human beings for that matter, but he believed strongly in the power of confusion.

"The more you don't get it, the closer you are to it. As soon as you start *understanding*, making *sense* of things, well César, that's where the real idiocy begins...."

Marcel had told César that he had etched each *X* himself with a kitchen knife. The first one when he moved into the place after his wife and daughter moved to Germany to make a family with another man and his teenage son.

5

After he had carved his first *X* just below the eyehole, Marcel would sometimes spend a good amount of time standing outside his door, admiring the new etching as if it was his very first tattoo. One day, his neighbor happened to come home during one of these moments of contemplation. Marcel's focus on the *X* afforded the neighbor a level of anonymity as he discreetly approached his own door, but just as the neighbor was turning the key in his door, Marcel looked over, transferring the intensity of his eyes onto him. The neighbor felt obliged to say something.

"*Bonjour,*" he said politely.

His neighbor waited patiently, leaving space for Marcel to say *Bonjour* back, but after the momentum of his own *Hello* waned, the neighbor began to turn back to his doorway. Suddenly, Marcel spoke up.

"I marked my door," Marcel said proudly.

The neighbor pulled his neck out of his doorway and peeked at the *X* carved on Marcel's door. "Oh, I see," he said.

Marcel's grin held solid. The neighbor felt obliged to compliment Marcel's effort. "Very nice," his neighbor said, then stepped into his apartment and closed the door.

About eight months later, the neighbor saw that the door had two Xs on it.

One evening, when both Marcel and his neighbor came home at the same time, the neighbor's eye lingered on the second X.

"The landlord..." Marcel inserted.

"Pardon?" the neighbor asked, caught off guard.

"Yeah, I know, the landlord insisted I carve another one in... 'cause he heard that the first one was so *nice*."

Marcel's sentence went into the neighbor's head like a piece of bread into water. He couldn't help but feel the obligation to compliment the second X, as he had complimented the first.

"*Very nice*," the neighbor said.

During the weeks that followed, whenever Marcel passed his neighbor, the neighbor avoided eye contact. Then the third X appeared. Not long after, the two bumped into each other on the stairs. It was just before Christmas, and the wooden stairway seemed to be charged with a silent childhood.

"Hey there," Marcel said.

His neighbor almost tripped over his step, his hand caught the railing.

"Oh, hello."

"Crazy, right?"

"Sorry?"

"My door, I mean. You've seen it."

The neighbor looked at Marcel silently.

"...I mean, you leave two *nice*-looking Xs alone for one minute and what do you know, you come home to a third!"

His neighbor stood still. His mouth opened, then closed, bewildered.

"Happy holidays," Marcel said and jumped down the stairs robustly.

6

After five years, there were five *X*s in a line down Marcel's door. The sixth *X* was considerably lower than the rest.

"My daughter did that one!" Marcel boasted to his neighbor, who at this point did his best to avoid engaging in any conversation with Marcel.

His neighbor had never seen a little girl coming in or out of Marcel's place. And the thought of giving a young child a sharp object to carve into a door with did not seem like good parenting. But above all, his neighbor did not want to get himself tangled in whatever was going on with Marcel and that door. So he said the thing that to him seemed to close the conversation the quickest.

"*Very, very nice…*" the neighbor replied and slipped into his own apartment, quickly shutting the door behind him.

7

Not too long after that, someone broke into his neighbor's place, and, like Marcel described, *picked the crumbs off the floor.* They even took the pens on the counter. Oddly enough, they left the objects of true value, the furniture, the electronics, the marble chess set untouched. In the end, Marcel was not sure why his neighbor even complained. It just looked like someone came in, cleaned the place thoroughly, and left.

"If they would have just taken something…" Marcel had overheard his neighbor saying on the phone in the stairway, "…if only they would have taken something valuable, well maybe then I could sleep at night!"

8

Marcel's neighbor filed a complaint concerning what he was calling a robbery. Although the list of missing items included: four pens, two to four various-sized scraps of paper containing notes, one tea-bag wrapping, a couple of stale sugar cubes, one beer can cap, the broken end of a keyring, two to three business cards lying around. From subsequent phone calls that Marcel overheard, he understood that the neighbor had gone to file a second complaint, concerning a young man he thought was loitering outside the building.

"I've no idea who this skinny kid thinks he is, standing like that against the tree, just looking at me with his creepy eyes...Yeah, I'm sure as hell he's looking at *me*, looking so hard I can see the exact color of those damned eyes of his.... They're...these peering eyes, like slivers, like dark marbles...!"

9

Now there were seventeen *X*s on Marcel's door. His neighbor no longer complimented them. In fact, Marcel didn't see much of his neighbor these days. But he knew he was still there. In the evenings, especially if Marcel stood quietly in his shower, he could hear his neighbor talking to someone on the phone through the wall. Some-times his neighbor yelled into the receiver, which made it easier to listen in. But sometimes he just whispered sloppily.

There were nights when Marcel was sure his neighbor was talk-ing to an ex-wife, as he spoke with outdated love like a telescope try-ing to find that rare star in the constellation.

"...The hell with it...Now at least we can say *Remember me*... Good thing you left me...otherwise I would've killed you. Haha..."

Other nights, maybe he was talking to someone else.

"Yeah, no, I'm okay. No, yeah, I'm okay..."

10

César knew Marcel's doorbell was long broken (maybe it never had worked). He rolled his fingers into his palm and brought his knuckles up to the space below the eyehole. Before he could touch the wood, the door clicked and pulled open.

"Just in time for fish!" Marcel said.

11

For a man in his sixties, Marcel was in very good shape. Not just physically either, although he did have a pull-up bar bolted in the doorway from the kitchen to the living room. His eyes had a sheen of perpetual delight. The look of a boy who's hiding a beetle behind his back.

They walked through the hallway and went into the office room.

"Take a seat!" Marcel said to César, and hopped over to the other side of the desk.

On the bookcase behind Marcel sat two framed photos of two girls. The younger girl was on the top shelf, with a thin, smart-aleck smile. Her eyes were forceful, certain. The older girl was on the shelf below, with her lips held together, not smiling. Her eyes now used their strength to push something away. César had always assumed these were Marcel's daughters, as both strongly resembled each other.

Marcel had the frames turned outward, so that they faced whoever was sitting in the chair in front of him. This gave the impression that no matter what he said, the two girls agreed with him.

Marcel drum-rolled with two fingers on the side of his desk. "*Manuel Rodriguez!*" he announced. "The role of a lifetime!"

"*Manuel Rodriguez,*" César repeated shyly.

"Big fish material, kid! Latino psycho type. You know better than I do, right?" Marcel gave a wink.

"…Latino psycho like…"

"Pepe Psicapato! Loco Nacho! Twisted in the head beneath his sombrero, you know…"

"…Twisted…like…how?"

"Come on, buddy. He's tracking down young women, some of them girls, innocent girls, pretty girls... He's tracking them down and...you know."

"What's he doing to them?" César was suddenly concerned.

"Oh, awful things. Disgusting things. *Areeeba areeeba*, right..."

César looked at Marcel, trying his best to understand. He glanced up and caught the two faces of the girls, one smiling and the other frowning. He was starting to feel uneasy. Marcel sniffed loudly, interrupting.

"The audition is tomorrow morning, so you gotta sink into this quick."

"Tomorrow? Really?"

"You think you can handle a macho muchacho like that? You know, a man who would do that...to young, innocent, pretty girls..."

"...I mean, I'd have to look at—"

"WHOA. Whoa whoa whoa." Marcel jumped. He grabbed the sides of his desk and pulled in towards César. "Buddy, please. Don't let me down here. You can't let me down on this one."

"I won't—"

"The thing is, I've already buttered up one of the producers about you. We're dealing with big fish here, for you and for me. You're *my man* here. You're *their* man. You're *the* man! Say it. Say it with me, buddy. Tell me. Tell me you're my loco nacho..."

César's mind began to race. Thirteen episodes. National TV. Wide distribution. DVD. Spanish subtitles. His family could see it in Mexico. His brothers. Tough guy. Scary guy. Psychos don't take *shit*. No one messes with a psycho. César suddenly felt so excited, the pinheads in his eyes sparkled feverishly, as if trying to become meteors. Marcel stared at him anxiously.

"I'M YOUR LATIN PSYCHO!" César roared.

Marcel smiled with so much tenderness, César almost called him *Papa*.

The two young girls stared down at César, one smiling and one frowning at his fate.

XIII

FOTOS

1

THERE'S A METAL RUMMAGING in the keyhole. A click and a clang and a chain dropping like a brass necklace. The door opens and the Head Natasha of the Natashas enters holding a large, padded book. All the Natashas perk up.

"Okay, girls, who wants to see some pictures?"

"Oh I do!" "I do." "I do…"

Each Natasha shouts out in her own way. Some quack out instantaneously, unashamed of their saliva. Others concentrate when they speak. They are concerned about their dignity and let their words out accordingly.

"Okay then, come around, come around."

The Natashas cluster around the Head Natasha. She crouches down and opens her wide, padded book.

2

First photo, full page, color:

Marilyn Monroe with her wrists pressed together, pushing up as if coming out of a pool. It is not clear whether she is actually at the pool because the background is completely black. Also, she's wearing a sleeveless powder-blue bustier of an elegant dress, the kind of garment one does not normally wear if they are at the pool. Her eyes gaze slightly beyond you. They skim over the hairs on top of your head. Her mouth is open but her teeth stay firmly pressed together.

"She sure looks nervous," the lanky Natasha says.

"Well, you'd be nervous too if all around you was nothing but black!" the sleepy Natasha replies.

The Natashas peer at this photo from all angles, elbowing each other to make room, some hovering on their tiptoes, others levering between ankles. The Head Natasha turns the page.

3

Two half-sized photos, color:

Marilyn Monroe has her arms up, hands on the back of her neck, as if holding up her hair. She is wearing a black turtleneck. Behind her, the wooden beams of an old barn. Maybe she's in Tennessee. Maybe there's a pig poking his snout at her leg. This we can't see, because the photo is just from her torso up. Her breasts push out in cones. Her mouth is open. She must be in the middle of saying something. Something like, "That light is in my eyes." Or, "The pig's got his snout on my leg." Or, "I don't think I like myself today."

Second photo:

Marilyn Monroe is in a black swimsuit, sitting in a chaise longue on a pool deck. One of her shiny legs is up in the air. She's holding the straps of a black heel upon her foot. She pulls down on the straps, as if hanging on, so that she won't blow away. However, there is no sign of wind. She is maybe saying something coquettish, like, "Come over here, you." Or sucking in air because of an acute pain in her uterus. Both produce very similar flirtatious sounds. No wonder the cameraman is confused.

One Natasha inhales until her stomach pushes over her jeans, then she seals up her lips and leans directly over the photo. The other

Natashas watch her. Suddenly, she lets her lips burst open and a gust of breath slaps onto the photo.

"Crazy, what're you doing!"

"I wanted to see if she'd move."

"It's a FOTO. Do you know what a FOTO is?"

"Yeah I know what a FOTO is."

"My cell phone takes FOTOS," the Natasha with freshly painted nails says.

"Who cares."

Another Natasha with scraped knuckles extends her long finger and points at everyone.

"There are FOTOS of you and you and you and you and you on the internet and let me tell you, you're not wearing much!"

"Those FOTOS are not for the clothes anyways, duh."

"Yeah, they are like doctor-visit FOTOS. You know, bend over, slide forward, spread your legs, relax."

"I would NEVER let no doctor or whoever take one of those FOTOS of me…without paying up front!" a Natasha says proudly. The Natashas behind her nod in solidarity.

"Um…I don't think…I want…like, one of those FOTOS… taken of me…at all." The new Natasha has watery eyes.

"Oh but you don't even need to be there really," the blue eye-shadow Natasha says kindly.

"A vacant house doesn't complain of a robbery," the redhead adds.

At this, a plump Natasha shifts her hips forward.

"Forget that. What are you, ashamed of your body? I'm not. I've got a delicious body." She moves in towards the sitting Natasha and circles her hips in front of her eyes. "I'm delicious, dee-lee-sush."

"Lemme see." Sunflower budges through the crowd.

"Stop pushing!"

"You smell!"

The rest of the Natashas start pushing and shoving and pinching each other, until the Head Natasha must interfere.

"Now, now, girls, let's not get too excited. It was already nice to look at those photos. Wasn't it? Wasn't that nice?"

"It was really nice," a Natasha states proudly.

"Really, really nice!" another adds.

"But now it's time for bed."

The Natashas huff and pout.

"Yes, yes, it's bedtime."

"O…kay…"

"There we go, that's my girls."

The Natashas file towards their spots and plop themselves down. One by one they burrow into their blankets and close their eyes.

"That was *so* nice…" they mumble drowsily.

When the door is closed and the lock is rebolted, the bodies of the Natashas are lifeless, like lumps of laundry. Each one breathes rhythmically, in and out. Between their breaths, odd sounds push out. Each Natasha reverts back to her mother tongue. She mumbles names. *Marta. Marilena. Mariya.* Ragdolls they once loved.

The saliva swooshes slowly back and forth in each mouth. One by one their saliva synchronizes with the rest. It forms the sound of a crashing wave, crashing onto the shore of a beach.

On that beach, Marilyn is sitting in the sand. She's wearing a red-and-white-striped bathing suit. Her knees catch the light. Her legs are slightly open. She crosses her arms over her breasts, squirming, right to left, left to right.

Relax, Marta.

Relax, Marilena.

Relax, Mariya.

You're only being tickled.

XIV
MANNY

1

FINALLY BACK IN HIS small apartment, César sat at his desk with the audition scenes on one side and his notebook on the other. *Manuel "Manny" Rodriguez.* This season's Latin psycho. César did have some experience with psychotic personas, even if it wasn't professional. Poor Estefania who married her sister's killer, Laura the beautiful grieving widow and naughty Dr. Arturo and his facial reconstruction, Doña Carlota, both jealous and protective of her young, horny niece. Enrique. Federico. Then all the men he played at his telemarketing job. Melancholic Andres, itchy-fingered Pablo, and of course Juan-Miguel the hothead.

César tried to bring Manny to life alongside these past characters, but Manny kept pushing away, standing to the side. He was starting to see it. Manny was different.

2

All his life, César had never doubted that he was an actor. He was sure of it the way he was sure he desired men even before he had ever kissed one. Although he hadn't ever landed a professional acting role, he had always thought of his childhood impersonations and his years at the acting school as a lifetime of acting experience.

Throughout those years, he felt there was no particular rush for a full-fledged career. He was content *to be an actor*, to find ways to practise this daily, even if no one else saw. All he wanted was to live as an actor, acting.

But as he contemplated Manny, he started to see that he had long outgrown these characters of his past. They were mere sketches, catchphrases, and anecdotes. At the acting school, all his work was caricatured, no matter how hard César had tried to give it depth. Whenever César had expressed to his teacher that he'd like to work on a "serious role," his teacher would lift his hand by his wrist and gesture a limp infinity sign.

"All roles are serious roles," the teacher would say as if he were speaking Latin.

César agreed in theory, but saw clearly in practise that his roles were always the gimmicky part of the scene, and any effort to give these roles sincerity was discouraged.

"César, are you trying to make a mess of these characters on purpose?" his teacher had once scolded him.

"I'm just trying to give them a soul..." César replied self-consciously.

"Well...looks like they don't want anything to do with your soul..." The teacher smiled, then looked back at his other students. Some of them laughed, and he felt rewarded.

When he saw the teacher in private and tried to explain more precisely his ambitions, the teacher recited other theoretically impenetrable phrases, then looked at César as if he were in the way of who he was really trying to look at. No matter what César said, he could not break through these *universal truths of the profession*. The more he responded to his teacher's definitive statements, the more the teacher grew irritated that this student couldn't accept his higher wisdom.

3

César pulled the pen out of his mouth and its ballpoint touched the dry, white paper. As the black ink bled the first dot onto the page, he began to walk into Manny's life. He scribbled memories, familial disputes, spans of solitude, intimate moments. He sketched Manny's world, how he saw it, how he absorbed it, how he became a part of it. He sneaked around Manny's childhood and grew up with him. He stood by Manny as he threw his fits. He withdrew with him into his teenage years. He sat in back on his Honda motorcycle and held on tight as they raced down Mexican Federal Highway 1 from Tijuana. He watched Manny drink belligerently on street curbs. He sat in silence at dawn with Manny. He walked various cities behind Manny's heavy steps.

Hours passed. He kept writing down all the visions he was seeing, a life he was suddenly a part of. His heart was pounding. His eyes were glazed. He lifted the pen from the page and put it back between his teeth. Manny was the most fascinating man ever to have entered his life.

Manny, my latin psycho.

Manny, my beautiful boy.

4

Notes on Manuel (Manny) Rodriguez
BABY MANNY

Born in Tijuana, Mexico.

Wait, go back: his mother. She's from the southern region of Mexico, near the Valley of Oaxacas. Her childhood—indigenous traditions, her grandparents, the People of the Clouds.

One day, out of nowhere, her mother leaves town. One day, out of nowhere, her father comes back to say he hopes she never turns out like her mother, then leaves town again. Her grandparents love her. But they are old. They pass on. People of the Clouds go back to the clouds. No more traditions. Fourteen, fifteen, sixteen, men keep coming by. Barely seventeen. First baby comes. Héctor. The father takes off. She's got something though. Other men keep coming. Second child, Graciela. This papa's gone too. Soon though another takes his place. "How's a beautiful girl like you all alone?" Then a third child comes along, Ignacio. Just as quick, this papa scampers. Another comes by. He says something like, "What kind of a woman lets herself live this way? You beauty." He says he'll take care of her. Out of his "care" the fourth child comes, Javier. Then suddenly, Jeckyll & Hyde. Goodbye romance, hello violence. She's pregnant with her fifth. He says something like, "That little shit ain't mine. You've been whorin it." Now her forehead has a glaze of sweat. She's got constant fever. Bully tries to kill the baby several times. Bully uses his fists. But she fights off his fists. That night she's strong, superhuman, the way a mother protecting her child can be. He says he's tired of her witchery, he takes all the money in the house and disappears. And fifth baby comes—despite all the efforts to beat it to death. Baby Manny.

The five children grow up in filth. Circus ways, spend a lot of time calling each other bastards (because none of them have fathers). Make up easily and laugh hard at each other's ugliness with devotion.

5

BOY MANNY

Boy Manny grows up getting into trouble. Especially with the men that come by for his mother. Little by little, he develops a dark vibe. Little by little, the men stop messing with him. Little by little, adults and kids alone start to be afraid of Manny.

Soon his own mama starts to flinch when he's around. She thinks maybe its her own fault, for pushing out a battered baby.

Manny can read her mind. He says, "Shoulda let dat peeza-shit pound me to death, Ma."

6

TEENAGE MANNY

Teenage Manny's got big dreams and a frightening smile. He gets his way. Fifteen and shows up one evening on a Honda motorcycle. Where'd you get that? His mom's new man asks him. Nona yer damn bizness, bitch, he mumbles. Mom's man puts down his beer. Mom's man swings hard at Manny. There's blood on the floor. Manny wipes his nose and gets his ass outa there. His Honda days begin. Rides home and if the man's around, he takes back off again. Sometimes he's gone for days, then weeks, then it's his birthday. Sixteen and he takes off on his Honda. Tijuana River Valley. Across the border. Hangs out at Imperial Beach. Then moves on to San Diego. Soon, his track record starts. He moves around. Goes East. Las Vegas. New Mexico. San Antonio. Florida. Traffic violations, vandalism, theft, burglary, arson, assault...

US patroller stops Manny. Tells him to step off his vehicle. Manny lifts up his seat as if he's getting off, but then just slugs the cop in the face. The cop falls over his own scrambling, right in front of the Honda. Before the cop can get up, Manny's revved up the bike. The cop looks up. Too late. Manny rides his Honda over the cop's arm and off, away. The cop's screaming in the background. Blood orange sunset.

Now the law's really angry with Manny. But he's hard to catch. He's not a US citizen. Plus, sometimes thugs want him on projects. Manny says "No thanks" every time. Manny don't work for nobody. If thug insists, Manny gets pushy. This way, thugs and cops alike don't like Manny. Women. That's another story.

7

EUROPE/WOMEN

Manny's fucked up so bad in the States that he's gotta get out now. He goes to Europe 'cause some girl says come to Europe. She's obviously in love with him and obviously had a father who did stuff to her, 'cause she puts up with all kinds of stuff from Manny. Even asks him to do it to her. When she asks, it makes Manny uneasy. Sometimes he does it and sometimes he says, "Leave me alone."

One night, a new girl keeps swirling on his lap. He's sitting outside the bar. She's trying to straddle him. "Yer fuckin up the view," he says, pushing the girl away. She takes off her shirt. She's topless and it's winter, but she doesn't feel the cold. She wants his attention. Manny just wants to look at the sky for a bit, alone. Watch the colors change. She keeps coming back. Manny keeps pushing her away. Until she doesn't stand up again. She's lying topless in the street, with her legs bent behind her.

Manny continues to sit there, watches the sky turn orange then blue then violet and takes swigs from the bottle. Then he stands up and leaves. The girl doesn't move.

8

PARIS

Manny ends up in Paris. How? Not important. Same old thing. It's springtime. He's walking around alone. If he sees an ant, he picks it up on his finger and walks around with it crawling on his hand for a while. Then he carefully sets it down, back on its path.

Manny's got a thing about ants. He doesn't like it when people step on them. All insects in general, but especially ants. As a boy, he'd be screaming NO SE SUBA A LAS HORMIGAS!! with his eyes almost popping out of that thin face as his mama's man stomped on the ant routes and laughed at the crying boy.

Fast forward. Manny's twenty-nine, and still has the same face as a teenager. He's sticking around Paris now. Why? Simple. He likes the skyline. But the problem is he can't stay out of trouble. In and out of police stations. Every time they have to let him go. "Ain't got nuthin on me, man, I'm as free as da fuckin birds all up in dat sky."

Back to the script: four girls have gone missing with same MO. Now a fifth's been found. Again, Manny's picked up by the French authorities. They are just itching to catch him for something. He's obviously "up to no good" anyway, obviously "better off the streets," obviously "safer for everyone if he's locked away." But proof, they need proof. Four girls. Now five.

Manny, did you do it?

Tell me.

My beautiful psycho. All alone in this world. No one believes you've got a right to live. Except for me, Manny. I do. I've never been happier since I met you.

9

César read over his notes. They felt like a pile of intimate love letters. Things he shared with Manny that no one else would know. It was true, no one else would or could know.

The actual information he received from his agent to prepare for the audition was quite sparse.

Manny is Latino (let's just say a criminal, the writer probably thought). Manny is complicated (let's just say psycho, the director simplified). Manny's charged with doing dark things to five young women (Oh, I know a good special effects makeup artist! the assistant most likely added). All the viewers want to see a guilty Manny, a beastly Manny, a punished Manny. But did Manny actually do those things?

(You'll have to wait thirteen episodes to find out.)

10

As César got into bed that night, he went over his mantra for tomorrow's audition.

Word that makes Manny feel in charge: *Bitch*

Word that makes Manny nostalgic: *Honda*
Word that pushes Manny over the edge: *Hormiga*
Bitch, Honda, Hormiga
Bitch, Honda, Hormiga
César pulled the blanket up to his ear and curled tightly into it. In the darkness, he quietly repeated the mantra with his softly closing eyes. He felt that Manny was in bed with him, holding him tightly, whispering lightly into his still-boyish ear.

Bitch, Honda, Hormiga

César smiled gently. Just as he drifted away, he whispered out loud: *Te quiero, Manny…*

At that moment, he felt a distinct wind blow into his ear canal and a man's gritty voice whisper back, *Te quiero, César.*

XV
THE WINDOW

1

BÉATRICE SANG TO HERSELF in a half-voice because it was so late. She was in bed, trying to understand her day. She had woken up with a strange urge to cough, then when she did, out had come a name. In the afternoon, she had gone looking for a dress for her concert and ended up in a stark boutique with a woman who listened to the radio between stations. There, she had found her dress. There, she had tried it on. There, she had looked exactly how she had always wanted to look. Then, there was the woman, the name. There she was, *Polina*. *Polina*. The name, like the face, ran through Béatrice's thoughts. *Do-bee do-bee doo…*

A shard of moonlight lay on her cheek. The rest of the room was a landscape of bulbous shadows. As she hummed, most of the sound remained in her throat. Only the faintest breath from the movement of the syllables escaped, and seemed to form shapes in the dimness around her. Polina's face returned to her. One eye, tilted and almost Persian. Eyelashes dark and stiff.

Polina was watching her.

Béatrice closed her eyes and felt quite strange in her body, as if she had gone to bed without undressing. She slid her hand beneath the covers and felt the warm skin of her stomach. She turned her head towards the window. She saw the bare branches in the night air. A wind blew and shook them. As they swayed, she thought she saw a shadow move across them.

Pogoulyim?

2

There was a knock on her door. The knob turned and let in a slice of light. A bare leg stepped in. For a moment, the figure did not advance. Béatrice waited.

"Bee...?" her sister's voice came. "Bee..."

"What's wrong?" Béatrice said.

"Bee...I can't sleep," Emmanuelle said like a kitten.

3

When Emmanuelle was a child, she went through a spell of bad dreams, which little by little discouraged her from the whole activity of sleep. She would sit in bed, her eyes gluey with fatigue, clenching her fists to stay awake. At the time, her parents had tried many things. Bedtime stories, nightlights, warm milk, change in routine, a safety blanket. Their father would sit in a chair at her bedside as her protector, *you can sleep now, honey, I'm here.* But he always fell asleep first and Emmanuelle would be left in the dark, clutching her blanket, staring at the silhouette-lump in the chair her father had become.

Emmanuelle's dream was always the same: A man dressed all in black with a black woolen mask climbs into Emmanuelle and Béatrice's shared room. Béatrice is not in her bed, because her bed is neatly made. As the man makes his way to Emmanuelle, she wakes up instantly at the disturbance of his footsteps. Emmanuelle immediately looks over at the door, ready to scream. Just as she is about to call out, the woolen man covers Emmanuelle's mouth with his leather-gloved hand. The man lifts Emmanuelle out of the bed with one easy gesture and pulls her so tightly against his stiff chest that she can barely twist, let alone try to get free. Just as the woolen man is about to take Emmanuelle away through the window, her father and her mother both walk through the door into the room. They look blurrily at her. Emmanuelle tries to call out to them, but her mouth is shut tightly by the man's hand. All she can do is snort through her nose repeatedly. Her parents' vision sharpens and they take notice of their daughter in distress. Her father and her mother both begin to raise their hands up slowly. Their muscles appear to still be asleep. As their hands rise, so do Emmanuelle's eyes. She follows her parents' hands with utmost devotion.

When her father's and her mother's hands reach the level of their ears, they come to a stop. Emmanuelle holds her breath. She locks her eyes on their white hands which seem to be floating in the darkness. They begin to rock, dipping slowly to one side, then to the other. Emmanuelle stares and stares as if trying to decipher a foreign symbol, but then she realizes. Her father and her mother are not telling the man to stop, they are waving her *goodbye*.

4

And so, for a while, Emmanuelle became a little insomniac. Her mother tried lavender extract on her pillow. She rearranged the furniture. She put thicker curtains over the window. Her father stayed by her side night after night. Still, Emmanelle's eyes sunk deeper and darker from the lack of sleep.

She refused to talk about her dream to anyone except her sister. And Béatrice knew just what to do to keep safe from such men. She let Emmanuelle climb into her bed and pull her in close.

"Bee..." Emmanuelle whispered.

"Yeah?" Béatrice replied.

"Where were you, Bee? Why did you let the man take me away..."

Béatrice paused. She inhaled, then on the exhale began to sing softly. She pulled her sister into her side and tightened the covers over them both.

"*Do-bee do-bee doo…*" Béatrice hummed.

Like a potion, the tune made Emmanuelle's eyes heavy and her breath slow.

"Don't let him take me away this time…" Emmanuelle mumbled as she drifted off to sleep.

"*Do-bee do-bee doo…*" Béatrice assured her.

Night after night, Béatrice sang to her sister and put her to sleep. Over time the dream left Emmanuelle and she regained her confidence in sleeping alone.

The sisters kept their secret. But once in a while, the nightmare came back to Emmanuelle, and when it did, she went back to Béatrice just as she had done in her childhood.

5

"Bee…"

Although Emmanuelle was now twenty-eight, she came into her sister's room that night and spoke with the same voice as the terrified and sleepless eight-year-old girl.

Béatrice pulled open the bedcovers and Emmanuelle climbed in. She curved her body inward and placed her face against Béatrice's bare shoulder.

"Sing me something, Bee," Emmanuelle mumbled into her sister's warm skin.

As Béatrice began to hum, Emmanuelle closed her eyes and wrapped her arm around her sister's waist. It wasn't long before both sisters were asleep.

In their sleep, in this quiet room at the top of house, Polina watched these two women over the bed. *Telo, Nomer, Chiffre, Youpka…*

XVI

BITCH. HONDA. HORMIGA.

1

IN THE NORTHWEST SUBURB of Paris, Neuilly-sur-Seine, the morning is quiet. César is walking through the empty, white streets, following the building numbers with his eyes. *Just don't overthink it*, he is telling himself as he walks up to the flat, gray building. He checks the plaque near the door for the Studio floor then buzzes in. *Second floor*, the doorphone spits out.

Upstairs, the tripod is set up, the assistant has made sufficient copies of the script, and the two technicians in loose black jeans are closing the shutters on one of the overhead lights.

2

A woman with long brown hair in a loose, silver silk blouse tucked into her high-waisted jeans is standing in the open door. As she takes a step back, her heels make a click sound on the floor. She gives César a half-hearted smile with her thin, raspberry-painted lips, then turns her head back to the man swirling the coffee in his small espresso paper cup and itching his graying sideburn.

"Marcel's kid's here," she says.

The director looks up. He glances at César's face, then takes a moment to review his body. He smiles, revealing two front teeth bent slightly into each other, as if he'd been punched in the face in his childhood.

"Well, well, looks like we got a little shit on our hands…bravo, Marcel," he says and nods as if Marcel were in the room.

"The lights are ready," a man says from the back.

"Did you mark the tape?" the assistant calls back, her voice with a tone of perpetual disappointment.

"Yep. Ready to roll," the man replies.

"Do you want a coffee or something," the assistant asks César.

"No thanks."

"Okay then, let's get you in here."

3

César sits down on the cold metal chair in front of the bare table representing the "interrogation room" for the audition scene purposes. The other actor, playing the detective, has his strong, wide back to César, facing the wall, quickly going over some voice exercises. "*Dee dee dee. Da Da Da. AH AH AH.*" The assistant comes up behind César and pulls his arms down to the back of the chair. César immediately pulls away, and turns around, startled. The assistant holds up the pair of handcuffs in her hand, sighs, and says in an annoyed tone, "It's part of the scene…"

César flushes with embarrassment and lets the assistant handcuff him to the metal chair. The woman rolls her eyes and twists César's arms down and around until his hands touch each other. She clicks the metal rings around his wrists and onto the bars of the chair. When the rings snap shut, the cuffs hit the bar they are attached to, sending a buzz up the chair. He instinctively jerks and the cuffs cut into his wristbone. César's elbow twitches in pain. He can feel the assistant growing irritated with him. His neck bends down apologetically.

"All righty, César, you ready?" the director shouts.

"…Yep," César replies quickly.

"Gérard…?" the director says to the actor playing the detective as he finishes his mouth exercises.

"BA BA BA ZA ZA ZA…" the actor inhales deeply and his shoulders rise. Then he exhales and his shoulders lower and open. "Brrrrrrr rrrrrrr rrrrrrrr." He does his last tongue rolls.

"*Prêt*," the actor pronounces in a solid, clear voice.

The director rubs his hands together then claps twice.

The man behind the camera shouts, "Rolling," and the assistant clacks the scene marker in front of César's face.

Just as César's nerves begin to rise, he feels a warm pressure on his back press gently in. *Te quiero, César…*

4

The actor playing the detective turns around. He is holding a beige file in his hand. He takes a step towards César. César's shoulders are hunched forward, his hands locked to the back of the metal chair. *Bitch. Honda. Hormiga.*

"We all have big ideas," the actor says in an even, controlled tone.

He leans down towards César's lowered head. "Wouldn't you agree, Mr. Rodriguez?"

César can feel the metal rings of the cuffs pinching his wrists again. He tries to move his shoulder blades to adjust the position, but no matter which way he twists, they press into his bone.

"Now, now, Mr. Rodriguez. No need to dumb yourself down. You're a smart man…"

Bitch. Honda. Hormiga. Bitch. Honda. Hormiga. César is trying to focus despite the pain coursing up his forearms.

"As a smart man, I know you've had a big idea at least once in your life. And what did you do when you had this big idea, well, you wrote that idea down. You wrote it down because you were sure it was an extraordinary, even brilliant idea. But, sometimes—and this happens to the best of us—when we go back and read our *brilliant* ideas later, we see that some of those ideas are in fact a little *stupid*. This can be very humiliating. What is one to do in these cases, Mr. Rodriguez?"

César blinks again to diffuse the pain.

"Well. We take that idea and we crumble it up and we throw it away, don't we? We have to get rid of this *stupid* idea to make way for a brilliant one. This is called having superior awareness and self-discipline. I highly commend anyone who can throw away a stupid idea."

César's eyes are starting to water. *Relax, César. Your line's coming up. Come on, you can handle a little pain...!*

"...It's the same way with people. Wouldn't you agree? Some people, we think, are extraordinary, brilliant! But then we look again, and with an admirable self-discipline, we see the truth. That they aren't worth a thing. And so, we crumble these people up and we throw them away. Isn't that what you're going about doing, Mr. Rodriguez? Getting rid of the world's stupidity? Making room for brilliance."

The detective opens the beige file he has been holding and pulls out a photo. He throws the photo onto the blank metal table, it lands like a flimsy slap. It's the body of a young woman, her face turned to the side, her mouth open. On her throat smudges in violet, midnight blue, and gas yellow. A landscape of toxic waste. Her skin is the color of diluted olive oil. Around her smooth, lifeless ear are strands of hair. The strands are thin, but long, and stick to her collarbone. Some even reach her ashen breasts.

César looks at the photo, then back up at the actor in the detective's uniform.

"Look familiar?" the actor playing the detective says. He throws down another photo. It lands on the edge of the first, diagonally. It's closer, more intimate, the woman's face turned to the left. Her cheek-bone protrudes, and a hollowness falls sharply to her jaw. The bones beneath her eyes are wide and the sockets are deeply set. The sides of her lips are whitish blue.

"Take a good look," the detective says.

He walks around behind César and places a hand on his shoulder. César is looking deeply into each photo. The pain around his wrists is fading away.

"Well," the actor says.

He pauses then throws down another photo. Kodak. The woman is in the street, wearing a short puffy jacket. It is zipped up, but ends at her waist. Her hair is parted in the middle, and hangs apathetically down either side of her face. Same face, those sharp cheekbones, and sunken eyes. Even with the makeup, she looks quite tired. Or else just Slavic.

"Like I said, Mr. Rodriguez, I commend you for seeing something for what it was really worth and crumbling it up and throwing it away. Now how about you tell me her name..."

César bends his torso forward, peering closer at the Kodak photo. *It can't be.*

"Wait, how...did you get this?" He whispers to the actor playing the detective. The actor raises his eyebrows and repeats his line.

"...her name..."

"I... I *know* her..." César whispers a little more pronounced.

The actor playing the detective glances at the director, then back at César.

"...Yes...you *do* know her."

"She was going to my school...then um...her grandfather died... he was Jewish so—"

The actor playing the detective coughs to cut César off, then raises his eyebrows at César. César squirms his back towards the director and whispers. "…She wasn't…garbage…she was going to be…important…she wasn't garbage—"

The actor playing the detective clears his throat.

"Wait." César stops. His eyes grow wide. "Oh!" He begins to whisper again, "Is she in the show…? She's in the show, right? I knew she would—"

The assistant sighs loudly, then mouths, "YOUR LINE..."

Bitch. Honda. Hormiga. César, get a hold on yourself, for fuck's sake!

"Oh. I'm sorry, I'm sorry," César mumbles and lowers his eyes.

The actor takes a step in, opens his chest and picks up the script.

"You want to tell me her name, Mr. Rodriguez..."

Marta? Marilena? Mariya?

Olya? Masha? Irina?

BITCH. HONDA. HORMIGA!

César raises his head and looks directly at the actor playing the detective. When their eyes meet, they hinge together. The two men stare at each other in silence, pushing deeper and deeper into each other's sockets. Suddenly, it is not two actors in the room anymore, it is a highly specialized detective and a Latino criminal. César tightens his jaw and pulls his chin towards the detective.

"Don't know diz bitch," Manny says.

5

The detective laughs with his mouth closed like he's trying to unplug his nostrils. When he's done, he cranes over to Manny's ear.

"You see, I think you *wish* she was just some *bitch*, to borrow your wording, Mr. Rodriguez, that's not the type of language I would use, but I'm quoting you, of course…I think you wish this *bitch's* face didn't *ring a bell*…but the thing is, Mr. Rodriguez, it does, doesn't it? This face right here, I bet it's ringing loud and clear. …ring…ring… ring…Well, aren't you going to answer it?"

Manny lifts his eyes to the detective. The detective frowns at the sight of him, like butter melting in the microwave. He starts pacing around the table, then stops at the wall of the audition room and lifts his chin, perhaps in an effort to look like Socrates. Indeed, with a Socratic air, he gazes into the wall as if contemplating the vastness of a sky held back by prison bars. (*Very nice*, the director notes.)

Manny snorts and the detective's contemplation on a man's freedom is interrupted. He turns around, keeping his head elevated.

"Anyway, Mr. Rodriguez, it's too late. Too late for what, you might be asking. Too late for *you*, Mr. Rodriguez. To put it briefly. To answer your question. So why don't you give me her name, and we can both stop playing dumb—so to speak. Of course, I'm sure you are a very bright young man... Do you understand what I'm telling you? Do you need a translator, Mr. Rodriguez?"

Manny flares his nostrils.

"Nah, man, I'm multilingual—just ask yer sisterz pussy HA HA."

The detective frowns. He goes back to the table and slides an open beige folder towards Manny. Inside, there are several documents. The detective slides them apart with his fingers.

"Take a good look..."

Manny lowers his eyes to the documents. The one on top is a form with a photograph stapled in the right-hand corner. The photo is of the same woman, except her eyes are open and darted forward as if trying to memorize a long number. There are words huddled together in some areas, then open spaces with clues printed in italics like whispers, *address, date of birth, social security number...*

"Can you read that name out loud for me?"

Manny cocks his head to the side.

"Are you literate, Mr. Rodriguez? I mean, can you read? *Vous pourriez me lire ce qui est écrit là-dessous?* Mr. Rodriguez. *¿Puedes leer?*"

"Ya, I can LEER, hombre. Peez-a-shit like me can even LEER LA BIBLE, put my derty tongue all ova God's werds mmmm. Ain't dat FUNNY? Why you ain't laffin, *bitch*?"

Detective drops his chin. "It's about time you show a little respect, Mr. Rodriguez. You're speaking to an officer of the law..."

"Yo, hombre, no problem, I gotchya. *Officer...BITCH!* HA HA!"

The detective's face remains unmoved.

"Wazamadder, you ain't got no senzo humor, DEE-TEK-TIV?"

"No, I suppose I don't, personally, but I've always appreciated a good sense of humor in others."

"Like yer mama?"

"Yes, my mother also appreciated a sense of humor, God rest her soul, of course."

"Dat why she had you?"

"Excuse me..."

"'Cause you so busted, I mean dat why she had you, so she could laff all day long lookin at yer busted face."

The detective approaches Manny. Their eyes meet, and they smile at each other. The detective chuckles. Manny gets ready to laugh his lungs dry. The detective's hand reaches around the back of his neck and slams Manny's face into the table. The chair Manny's cuffed to tilts forward, then thumps back down. Manny's cuffed hands flinch from the shock, then ball up into fists. He shakes his fists in the confines of the metal circles, bruising a ring around his wrists. Blood from his nose stains the documents of the nameless woman.

6

César's nose throbbed. He turned back around him to the camera on its tripod, behind which the cameraman looked at César annoyed. As a boy, this cameraman had looked through the lens of a coin-operated telescope for the first time while visiting a state park in

California. He saw as close as his own nose, a cliff-side full of crying sea lions. Now, he sees the same crying sea lions piled upon a rocky isle. He calls them actors.

César glanced past the cameraman over to the assistant. She was holding the script at her side and staring at him with the same eyes his mother had when she thought he would say the word "homosexual" out loud. César could see behind her, like an echo of her mood, the other crew people, all looking on with lukewarm interest. Everyone except the director, that is. The director had a wide grin on his face, showing off his two twisted front teeth.

The director began to nod enthusiastically, then he lifted his hand and added a quick spinning wrist. The zest made César flinch. "GOOD. GOOD. KEEP GOING," the director mouthed.

César licked a droplet of blood off his top lip. Iron and lemon rind gathered on his tongue.

"But...I'm bleeding," César whispered.

Yer doin good... a gritty voice said. *Keep goin, César. Yer da only one I have in diz world...*

7

"Ring...ring...ring..." the detective yells into Manny's face.

The detective flaps the folder against Manny's nose.

"Ring...ring...ring...! It's for you, Mr. Rodriguez. Aren't you going to pick it up...?"

Manny twists his face away from the slapping folder.

"What's the matter, Mr. Rodriguez, cat's got your tongue?"

"Cat ate my tung," Manny grits.

"I suppose there it is again, your fine sense of humor. I do appreciate it, except the problem I have here, Mr. Rodriguez, is that you seem to be looking for trouble. Am I correct? Are you looking for trouble, Mr. Rodriguez?"

"Nah man, I'm cool."

"It doesn't appear that way…on the contrary, it appears that you are looking for trouble. Didn't your mother teach…As they say in your culture: *No andes buscándole los tres pies al gato, Don't go around looking for three feet of the cat.* Remember your culture, Mr. Rodriguez? The one you spoke to ask for a drop of milk. Didn't your mother tell you then not to go looking for the three feet of a cat?"

"I was lookin for da *GATO* who ate *mi lengua.*"

"Oh Mr. Rodriguez, it's time you take responsibility for yourself. Don't you think your mother would be ashamed to hear you blaming cats for what you, *yourself,* have done…"

"Shutdafukkup 'bout my ma."

"Okay, okay, easy. I think I understand."

"You dunno shit."

"Hear me out, I think I do. I see how it is… Maybe as a kid you weren't given what every kid deserves to get. And that's not fair. You reached out for your mother's breast, and it wasn't there. Why did some kids get a breast full of warm milk, and you, just cold air?"

"Why you talkin 'bout my ma's titty?"

"I'm talking about more than *your ma's titty,* so to speak —again that's not language I would personally use, but—circumstances permit. I'm speaking of *love.* You know what *love* is, Mr. Rodriguez?"

"Sure do, hombre. *Love* is when da chica don ask fer money at da end, HA HA."

"You see, it's perfectly natural that you provide me with such an answer. It only goes to further prove the point I am trying to make. So let me be the first, and I am sure that I am indeed the first to tell you this. I'm sorry, Mr. Rodriguez. I am sincerely very, very sorry that you never got your mother's breast when you reached for it. You were only a baby, with a little, dry throat."

"Fuck, man, you talkin extra-nada-bullshit now."

"Every baby mouth deserves their mother's teat. It's only natural. But you pursed up your baby lips and got nothing at all. It was not your fault, Mr. Rodriguez. You needed your mother's breast and you didn't get it. So you continued grabbing. Pure instinct. Any animal would have done the same. Your mouth and your hands were only part of nature, weren't they? That's why you kept on grabbing. Because you were still that baby thirsty for your mother's milk. And to me, that is a very sad image. I tell you, when I think of it, I am almost moved to tears."

"Whachou talkin about deetektiv, I got my ma's titty."

"You mean you *were* breastfed, Mr. Rodriguez?"

"Sure waz, and ma wazent shy neither. She gave it away to a buncho oder babies fore me. I got broders and sisters even uglier dan me, HA HA."

"I see. Well."

Just as Manny tries to add a smart word, the detective grabs his chin and squeezes his jaw open. Manny jerks his hands but they are handcuffed to the back of the chair he's sitting on.

"Le-g-ovme," Manny jumbles between the detective's hand.

"Now, listen to me, Mr. Rodriguez. I know this must hurt, my thumb, pressing in the hinge of your jaw like this. I have to resort to these semi-barbaric ways, because there is quite simply no other manner with which to make you understand. You took milk from a good woman and made it bad. Do you understand the repercussions of such an act? There are babies who deserved to have that milk. These babies could have grown up to win the Nobel Prize...You've done something unforgivable, Mr. Rodriguez. You've spoiled good milk. So now, we are going to leave the *gato* and your jokes out of it, and you are going to pay your dues, Mr. Rodriguez, you are going to say her name."

Manny's face is turning red. The veins in his neck pulse and he releases a muffled whimper.

"You're going to say her name now, Mr. Rodriguez, because *you* were the one who took this name away from this world."

The detective squeezes the points of his cheeks in so they splurge into Manny's teeth.

Ah'wa —Yes good—*aaaa*—*tishhh*—Good very good— *Aaawaawawa*—*A A A*—*AAAAAAA*—*Achachach*—*ASH!* That'a boy —*ashashashnash*—Yes?—*Shashashasha*—Yes?—*Tatatatata*—Yes yes yes?—*NnnnnnnnnATaaaaSHa, NNTTAshhhhhhA*—

"NATASHA IS HER NAME!" César is screaming.

The detective purrs in the back of his throat.

8

"Shhh, César…"

César stopped screaming. He looked blankly at the actor playing the detective.

"You…mean…*Manny*," César whispers to the actor playing the detective.

The detective reached out to César, touching his shoulder, smoothing his hand down to César's bicep, then down to his twisted forearm. His voice was as soft as a boiled fish as he whispered to César, "Marcel was right about you."

"He was?"

"Yes…you're perfect for this."

9

In a room with no windows, the young woman stands with one hand on the wall, her fingers delicately touching the concrete. The cheap satin nightie she is wearing is rolled down to her hips, leaving her chest bare. Her breasts are small and firm, as if holding resentment. Her skin is a faded tea-color. She is looking at the concrete wall as if looking through a window. Her eyes glide slowly back and forth across one sharp crack within the cement.

Behind her, a woman stands holding a purple plastic hairbrush. The woman is brushing her hair and singing. *¿Qué he sacado con la luna ay yai aye...*

The young woman's satin nightie shifts on her hipbones as she breathes. Her eyes continue to glide across the crack in the parched wall. Through the crack, she is watching a young man. He is sitting down, his hands cuffed behind him to the chair. His head is hung over his shoulders. A drop of blood falls from his nose. It rolls down her cheek like a tear. The woman behind her keeps brushing her hair and singing. *¿Qué he sacado con la luna ay yai aye.* What have I gotten from the moon, aye aye aye.

¿Qué he sacado con el lirio ay yai aye. What have I gotten from the lily, aye aye aye.

¿Qué he sacado con la sombra ay yai aye. What have I gotten from the shadow aye aye aye

ay yai aye
ay yai aye

XVII
LET'S GO FOR A WALK

1

BÉATRICE STOOD AT HER bedroom window. She looked back across the dark room at her sister, fast asleep, hair streaming across the pillow. She turned back to the window. "Hello?" she said without thinking.

Something was in her hand. She brought it up to the moonlight and saw that she was holding a cell phone.

She listened. The static was the sound of pencil lead.

2

"It's Polina," said a voice through the static. Béatrice felt the velvet and coal tones graze over her neck. She leaned her head to the side, examining the sensation.

"The dress looks very nice on you, Béatrice," Polina said.

Béatrice looked down. She was wearing the black lace dress over her naked body. When did she put it on? Had she worn it to bed?

Béatrice looked through the window, at the yard below. Outside, the trees jabbed into the air in various directions. The ground was full of shadows.

"Do you see me, Béatrice?" Polina asked.

She scanned the shadows for Polina. She saw the darkened flowerbed. The pebble path. The rust-dry earth.

"No. Where are you?"

The receiver filled with static again. She pulled the phone away from her ear and lowered it to her side.

"Polina?" she said into the window. Her breath fogged the glass. "Polina?"

Béatrice...

"Yeah."

Come down, Béatrice. Let's go for a walk.

3

In the garden, shadows overlapped on the ground like misshapen fingers covering eyes. Béatrice stood between two shadows, in a crevice of light. The moon made her white skin glow beneath the black scales of the dress.

It was already October and the air was full of moisture. It made Béatrice's skin feel like clay.

Béatrice turned her head, peering carefully through the dark for Polina, but everything was as quiet as a pencil drawing.

She was not sure how long she had been standing there, waiting for Polina to come. A wind blew through the garden and Béatrice crossed her arms beneath her breasts and squeezed in, warming herself. Her breasts rose beneath her forearms as bathwater rises when a foot steps in.

A foot stepped in. Polina's.

Polina's hair was spread over her shoulders and looked almost as dark as her eyebrows now against the beige trench coat. Her lips had a joke playing across them.

"Well, do you see me now?" Polina said.

4

"Touch me. Make sure I'm real," Polina said.

Béatrice took a step forward. She extended her hand and grazed her fingertips down the stiff fabric of Polina's coat.

"That's my coat. It's real. Now make sure *I'm* real."

Béatrice extended her hand again and let it hover in the air. Only Polina's face and neck were uncovered. Even her hands were in her pockets. Polina leaned her head back, stretching her neck towards Béatrice like a bow. Hesitantly, as if asking for permission, Béatrice ran her finger down Polina's throat.

"I think you are real," Béatrice said.

In the darkness, the two women looked at each other.

"I hope you're right, Béatrice…"

5

Béatrice followed Polina to the end of the garden. When Polina opened the gate, Béatrice stopped, suddenly self-conscious. She looked down at her own body, her bare skin tightened under the lace.

"I can't go out into the street, I'm…naked."

Polina reached out and took Béatrice's hand. Béatrice felt herself surrender and be carried away. She had never given a part of her body like this to someone.

The streets were empty. No one walking. No one opening a door. No one lighting a cigarette. All the windows had thinly stretched eyelids. Even the parked cars seemed to have their eyes closed.

Here, outside the city, the suburban sky spread more generously and sagged against the rooftops as if it were longing for news.

It was no use asking where they were going. The answer didn't matter. What mattered now was suddenly so simple. It felt good to have her hand held by someone. Her whole body could relax and trail as if it were the end of a scarf, held upon Polina's neck and the wind.

She felt her eyelids close, loose and warm, until she was walking in darkness.

Polina's hand shifted and swayed as they walked. Gently, solemnly, like a small boat upon the sea. It held her afloat. It floated her forward.

*Bolina...*Polina hummed.

*Bolina, Bolina...*Béatrice hummed.

The two women walked, one leading the other.

Have you ever been sailing, Béatrice...?

6

When Béatrice opened her eyes, she was no longer walking, but lying down. Her white blanket covered her body and her head was set neatly upon her pillow. She was in her bed, in her room, in that old storage space at the top of the house. She looked up at the darkness above her and followed the foggy light towards the window. There was a shift in the room.

Béatrice remembered that evening, her sister's small voice and frightened eyes, she remembered singing and Emmanuelle's silky, warm head resting on her neck.

She rolled her head on the pillow to the other side of the bed and saw that the blanket had been pulled up at the corner, revealing empty, rippled sheets. Emmanuelle had gone.

She looked back across the room, her focus softening in the dimness. There was Polina, standing framed by the window.

7

Béatrice tried to sit up to see better, but felt something constrict her. She pulled back her blanket, and saw that she was still wearing her long, stiff black lace dress. From the window, Polina turned to face Béatrice.

"Do you want me to help you...?" Polina said.

Béatrice looked in her direction, but could only see the outline of her body. "Help me...?" Béatrice asked.

"Help you get out."

Even in the darkness, Béatrice could feel Polina's sliding smile. When she came up to the bed, Béatrice could now make out the beige color of her coat. But when she looked up at Polina's face, she could only see contours in the dimness.

8

"Here," Polina said. "Turn onto your stomach."

Béatrice slid herself onto her stomach, and turned into the white sheets. She lifted herself onto her forearms and her shoulder blades jutted out, against the lace fabric.

"Relax," Polina said and gently moved Béatrice back down, flat upon the bed.

Polina's hand moved towards Béatrice's neck. Her fingertips touched the collar of the dress where the zipper was and began to pull it down. Béatrice could feel the ridges separate from each other. Little by little, the dress spread open and curved out.

Polina put her hand flat on Béatrice's bare spine. Béatrice closed her eyes and absorbed the feeling of her hand. She inhaled and the air filled her lungs so that her back rose into Polina's hand, into the highways tracing her palm.

Polina lifted her hand and took an open edge of the dress with her fingertips. She peeled the dress off one shoulder. Then the other.

Béatrice turned over to face her and sat up. The dress sloped down at her collarbone, half undone, and clung to the tops of Béatrice's breasts.

"May I see them now?" Polina said.

9

Béatrice rolled the dress down to her waist. Her breasts were glowing white like the sheets, blankets, and pillows on the bed.

She lay back down onto the pillow and turned her head to the side, half-timid, half-alluring, so that only one eye was looking up at Polina.

"Do you like them?" Béatrice asked.

Polina reached out and traced their curves. She slid her fingertips down in a soft rhythm over their petal-like skin.

"You are real as well, Béatrice," Polina said.

10

Polina reached down to touch Béatrice's face. She stroked her ear, then brought Béatrice's face forward.

Face to face, Polina kissed Béatrice.

11

"I want to see your body," Béatrice said.

Polina looked up.

"Will you show me?"

Polina stood up from the bed. She stepped back into the darkness. Béatrice heard the stiff cotton fabric moving, then she felt the coat fall to the floor.

12

Polina stood naked at the side of the bed. Her arms were loose at her sides. Béatrice sat up and moved closer to see. She observed the dark clouds upon Polina's skin. She grazed her fingers over Polina's stomach, then the curve of her breast, then down her waist, then her hip bone. Polina turned around, and Béatrice continued. Her back. Her tail bone. The curve of her butt cheek. The plane of her thigh. Polina turned back around.

13

The skin everywhere on Polina's body was bruised. Across her

pubic bone, like a constellation, were tiny wounds, inflicted and re-inflicted, closed over, reopened and closed over again, the skin tough-ened into small scars. Béatrice's hand dropped into the darkness.
Polina drew back a mesh of her hair behind her ear with her fin-gers. For the first time, Béatrice could see what she may have looked like as a little girl, quiet, careful, and all-knowing.

"Nothing hurts," Polina said.

Béatrice reached up and pulled Polina towards her. Their faces pushed into a depth their kisses chased after.

14

Polina's cheek came down onto one of Béatrice's bare breasts. She licked the nipple there slowly in a circle. Béatrice felt her pelvic muscles pull through her, all the way down, as if trying to pull the tip of Polina's tongue there.

Béatrice took her hand and guided it between her legs, then took her own hand and smoothed it up Polina's thigh and slid inside. Po-lina tightened around Béatrice's fingers and pushed her own deep inside Béatrice.

Out of the darkness, Béatrice and Polina inhaled so deeply that they thought the whole room would be sucked in and crumbled be-tween their mouths. All their muscles clenched into their roots.

They grabbed each other's backs with their fingers and palms and nails and held on as tightly as they could.

15

It was almost dawn, but the two women lay in bed together, quietly giggling. Béatrice ran her fingers over the scars on Polina's pel-vis and whispered, *Nothing hurts*. Then Polina smiled and whispered back, *Nothing hurts*.

Nothing hurts.

Nothing hurts.
Not waiting or wishing,
Not touching or kissing,
Not asking or needing,
Not breathing or pleading.
Not thinking or speaking,
Not aging, or receding!
Nothing hurts!
Nothing hurts!
Nothing hurts!

The two women chanted joyfully together until the sun began to rise and a small black bird on the branch outside opened its short beak and began to sing the first note of morning.

At the sound of the bird, the two women's voices turned into a murmur.

Except for—
Re…mem…ber…ing. Re…member…ing. Remembering.
Their eyes closed and they fell into a peaceful sleep.

XVIII

BOLINA, BOLINA

1

THE HEAD NATASHA PUTS the heavy chain with the keys on it back into her pocket. She steps into the center of the room. All the Natashas have been waiting for her.

"Okay, girls—who here has ever been sailing?" the Head Natasha announces.

All the Natashas rub their tongues back and forth in their mouths as they think.

"Me!" the lanky Natasha exclaims. "…I think…"

"You're not sure?" the Head Natasha asks.

"Well, I mean I couldn't really tell 'cause I was sorta laying down in that space you know…below the floorboards."

"Oh yeah, I know that space…" the red-nailed Natasha nods, "but my boat was like a fancy boat."

The Natasha with milk crust on her lips butts in. "No way, no how honey, keep dreamin. No one puts something dirty on a clean floor, know what I mean."

"She's gotta point…" Natasha says, holding her journal.

"Wait, I believe her, it's SCIENCE. Sounds sound differently according to the space they're in. That's what EINSTEIN said," says another Natasha in a British accent.

"Einstein did not say that…"

"Einstein was a Jew!" the lanky Natasha squeaks, "…like me!"

"…It's in the books, like Sputnik, anyways that's how Vasya got into space and howled at the moon like it was a she-dog…"

"You're a she-dog," the sleepy Natasha drones.

"Least I was brought in on a fancy boat, you're just jealous 'cause they had to wrap you in a carpet and stuff you like a roll in the back of a truck for nine hours. Then, you were so dumb, you cried and cried 'cause you thought you'd never be able to walk again all 'cause you couldn't feel your legs! But after a couple days, the feeling in those legs came back. See, this is what I mean, you don't even know how the musculatory system works!"

Natasha daggers her finger forward and announces, "Well, you're so stupid, they told you you'd go pick oranges in su-sunny Turkey for a thousand dollars a month, and now you're su-stuck in this pit and you got people pickin YOUR oranges and it's basically FREE, good thing too 'cause they're r-r-r-ROTTEN!"

Natasha's pupils dilate.

"Oh! Well! They promised you'd dance at rich-people tables, but after they saw your *Baba-Yaga body*, they decided you're better face-down lik'an old rug!"

"Talk 'bout old rugs! You're so *worn out*, they make you lie down, then get a fresh girl on top, so *she* won't get dirty."

"Yeah, well you're so dirty, they had to leave you in the river to soak, *permanently!*"

"Oh shut it, you're the one with bleeding gums."

"Yeah, that's gross."

"Least I'm not *vulgar*."

"OH—*you're* so *vulgar*, they had to tie your legs together so you'd quit airing it out!"

"And you-you-you're so *ugly*, they were throwing a fist or two at your face, hoping to fix it up!"

"*You're* so ugly, they had to move on to your sister!"

"…Then they realized it runs in the family!!"

"HA HA HA."

"And that's why they had to zap your babies, the world can't handle any more of *that* face."

"Zap zap zap!"

"Look who's talking, they scraped you clean like a melon, and now you don't even get your periods!"

"What's so good about periods? Don't get time off for 'em anyways. They're just a pain in the uterus!"

"You're so stupid you don't even hear yourself. If you don't get your periods, that means you're not a LADY anymore!"

"Yeah, least I'm still a LAY-DEE…"

"Me too!"

"You—you're just…"

"…an old rug!"

"Stinky laundry!"

"A mushy orange!"

"Girls, girls!" The Head Natasha raises her hands in the air, then brings them to her temples. "You're giving me a headache."

All the Natashas sink their eyes down to the floor.

"Okay, okay, don't pout. Now. It's obvious none of you have ever been sailing because in order to go sailing you need a rich boyfriend. Bowl of fresh grapes on the deck. Designer bikini. No bruises on your body. No ingrown hairs. No scratched-off scabs. Get what I mean, ladies?"

"Yeah, oh yeah, that sounds really nice."

"Anyway, you don't know this 'cause none of you have been sailing before, but when you are sailing, you need to pay special attention to the wind. I know because I've been sailing."

"You have, you really have?"

"Yes I have."

"Oh, tell us, please tell us what it was like!"

"Did you have a rich boyfriend?"

"Yes I did."

"And did he have chest hair?"

"Lots."

"And a gold chain?"

"Two! One with a cross and one without."

"What was his name?"

"Yeah, was it Pasha, the one who collects our cash?"

"Or Igor, the one who keeps an eye on us from his car?"

"Or Vadim, the one who settles things with the police?"

"Or Kyrill, the one who smacks us around when we make a fuss?"

"No, no, we're getting off subject. Pay attention, what I'm telling you here is important. The wind is everything when you sail. Stronger than all the *cash* in your boyfriend's pocket. And the *hair* on your boyfriend's chest. And the *gun* in your boyfriend's waistband. Get what I mean, ladies?"

"Yeah, oh yeah, the *wind* sounds really nice!"

"It is. And if you pay attention, you'll know when you need it. And when you need it, you'll know to call it. Otherwise you might get stuck in a real shithole situation."

"Oh, we know all about shithole situations."

"Yes, I've no doubt you do. Because you don't know a thing about sailing."

"So…how do you call for the wind?"

2

All together the women repeat after the Head Natasha: *Bolina, bolina, bolina…*

"No, no, wait hold on," the Head Natasha interrupts the girls mid-vowel. "You have to say it *without* saying it."

All the Natashas look at each other to see if there is one among them who understands.

"Go ahead, girls, *say* it…but *don't* say it…"

Each Natasha tries on her own to say it without saying it. They open their mouths. They twirl their tongues, this way, that way. They pull their cheeks, down, up. They scrunch their lips to their noses. Some lips smack. Some spit by accident. Some just make slurping noises.

"HEY, I think she's got it!" One Natasha jumps up.

All the Natashas look at the girl near the wall. Her arms hang at her sides. There is a cigarette still burning in between her fingers. The smoke rises like a stream alongside her waist, and the tobacco chitters and burns up to her fingertips. Then this Natasha starts lifting her hand upwards, trailing the smoke up with it. Her eyes stare fiercely ahead, with her cheeks sucked in and her lips puckered in the shape of an X.

"Look, look, look, the smoke is white!" a Natasha yells.

"Like the sky in Moldova…" the lanky one blurts out, then covers her mouth.

"Like the bottle of milk, *moloko*…" the round-faced Natasha admits.

Then there is a sort of draught, as if the room itself took a breath. Through the passage of air, a voice floats through, from years ago. *Like the white rose, the white rose…* The Natasha near the wall is still as a statue, with one arm in front of her head as if calling out to someone. That hand still holds the burning cigarette between its fingers. Suddenly, her fingers move, as if to wave. At this, the cigarette falls from her fingers and the white smoke is blown into her in a gust. Just as soon as the smoke passes through her body, there is no body at all.

The Natashas stare with big eyes, then a mild voice comes from the crowd.

"You think she's gone sailing?"

XIX

FRIDAY

1

When Béatrice woke up that morning, she looked over expecting to find Polina there. To her surprise, the space was empty. When she lifted the covers, she saw that she was naked and there neatly laid out alongside her was the black lace dress.

She looked to the window, expecting to find Polina standing there. But saw just the white morning light patterned with the bare branches, upon which that small, crooked-neck bird sat. It had stopped singing and was now holding its marble-eye steadily on Béatrice.

Béatrice stood up and was startled by her own body, which felt intensely present. She got up on her feet and felt her legs straighten and her back align and her shoulders descend. She walked around her room with these new sensations, gradually realizing that they were hers. She went back to the window and opened it. A chill autumn air floated through. *Where was Polina?*

Béatrice put on a white bathrobe from her closet and wandered out of her room barefoot, down the sanded stairs, into the silent house. She walked past Emmanuelle's room, her door was ajar. She looked in, no one. She opened the bathroom door, no one. She walked through the hallway and down the stairs. She looked around the living room, her parent's room, the second bathroom, out into the garden. No one.

Emmanuelle must be at her hospital residency, her father at one of his carpet boutiques, her mother out shopping for this or that. She added up the absences and concluded the house was empty. She stepped into the kitchen for a glass of water and there she was.

"I didn't want to wake you," Polina said. She was sitting at the kitchen table, her beige coat buttoned all the way up and tied at the waist.

Béatrice's hands flinched up and closed the white robe.

"Am I frightening you, Béatrice?"

"No," Béatrice said blankly.

"What is it, then?"

Béatrice remained silent. She looked at Polina, trying to understand how this woman who seemed to belong to another side of the day was suddenly here again, in her worn, childhood home.

"Well, I won't keep you," Polina said to break the silence.

"From what?"

"From getting ready. It's your big day."

Béatrice remembered it was Friday. The day of her concert.

"It's just a concert, it's nothing."

Polina smiled.

"Nothing's nothing. *My beautiful woman,*" she said and got up. She opened the door, then turned back towards Béatrice. "*A ce soir,*" she said then closed the door behind her.

Béatrice went upstairs to her room and turned on the keyboard. A breeze from the open window blew a strand of her blonde hair loose. It swept across her cheek, as thin as an ant's antenna. She swept the strand back, then sat down on the piano seat and placed both hands on the keys. Her finger mindlessly pressed down on a note and a sound ran out like a mouse. She ran her finger a bit further down and pressed a B flat. A fatter mouse scrambled out.

She opened her mouth hesitantly, and waited for her voice to come. Her voice did come. But not in a song. One word.

"Polina."

Then a feeling between dream and memory. Polina in the yard. Polina leading her by the hand. Polina kissing her breasts. Polina pushing deeply inside her. Polina, this morning, sitting so starkly at her kitchen table. *No, you are not frightening me*, Béatrice thought. She placed her fingertips on the keys and began to sing, as if into Polina's ear.

2

Béatrice came downstairs to the kitchen and poured herself a tall glass of water which she drank in one steady gulp. She got out a jar of honey and scooped out a teaspoonful. She placed the teaspoon on her tongue and let it dissolve down her throat.

A hand tapped on the glass door that led out to the yard. She felt an excitement travel through her. *Polina!* She turned around with the teaspoon still in her mouth and looked straight at the window. The sight made her cough and the teaspoon fell out and hit the floor. It was Jean-Luc. He was waving. Béatrice bent down and picked up the half-honey-covered teaspoon and went to the door. She turned the knob and stepped back, letting him in.

"Emmannuelle's at the hospital."

"Oh. Yes, I thought she might be…You ready for the concert tonight?"

"Not much to do. Just get up and sing."

"Glad that it's not too stressful. I can't imagine having to stand up in front of all those people. But then again, I guess when you have something *special*, it's nice to…*share* it…no?"

Béatrice smiled slightly. Then frowned slightly. Then straightened out her lips.

"You're such a…closed-off person, Béatrice, you know? Never mind."

They stood face to face. Béatrice turned and put the honey-coated spoon she was holding in the sink.

"So, you are going to wear that dress tonight? The new one," Jean-Luc said.

Béatrice turned on the faucet, picked up the sponge, and washed clean her spoon. When she turned around Jean-Luc was in the same spot, staring straight at her.

"It looks great on you," he added.

Béatrice felt her cheeks stiffen. She turned back to the sink.

"The dress."

Béatrice turned the water off and stood with her wrists on the sink's edge, hands hanging towards the drain. Jean-Luc took a step towards her. The fingers of her still wet hands curled in and her eyes closed. Béatrice wished he would just leave. He shouldn't have been there. It was Polina who should be standing behind her now, not some man who had attached himself to her sister and hung around all these years, intruding upon her.

"You look...very...very...nice...in it," Jean-Luc said to Béatrice's back.

Her fingers gripped the sink tighter. "I know," she said through her teeth.

Jean-Luc remained where he was and watched Béatrice like a screw turning slowly into wood.

"...Well, maybe I'm making you uncomfortable. I just thought I'd stop by. Anyway, see you tonight then."

Béatrice opened her eyes.

"Okay. Bye," she said, without turning around.

"Bye, *Miss Monroe...*"

Jean-Luc closed the door behind him.

3

Béatrice snapped around and ran to the door, pulled it open, and stepped outside. Jean-Luc was just closing the gate from the yard on to the street.

"What did you say?" she yelled.

Jean-Luc turned his head, startled. In all the time he had known Béatrice he had never heard her raise her voice, let alone yell. Jean-Luc suddenly felt a bit stirred.

"What did you call me?" Béatrice repeated.

He put his forearm on the top of the gate, and leaned his hip in. He didn't say anything because he didn't need to. Life is delicious when you've made a beautiful woman yell for the first time.

Béatrice felt her heart speeding up. Her chest rose and fell, rose and fell.

"Don't call me that," Béatrice said.

4

When Jean-Luc was a boy he had an aunt who always showed up at their house with eyes that looked as if she had spent the whole day crying. She'd sit at the kitchen table and his mom would make her a coffee and bring her an ashtray. Normally smoking in the house wasn't allowed. But when this aunt came around, the rules changed. She had wrinkled eyes (from all that crying), but otherwise a fit body for her age, with exquisite, full breasts. She must have been well aware of this feature, for she always wore blouses which displayed them proudly, and little Jean-Luc would look at them shyly.

This aunt could not shake the habit of giving herself wholly to men who degraded her, physically or emotionally (as Jean-Luc's mother put it). The ritual was the same. She would come in with those gutter eyes and cradle her coffee and puff one cigarette after another as she recounted each story as if nothing of the sort had ever happened to her before. Then, something would turn, her eyes would dry up, and her lips would stiffen. This was what Jean-Luc perceived to be the revenge phase. Yet it was not quite revenge. It was merely the moment when, from the swampy tragedy of her circumstances, a gulp gave way to a hand, a bone-stiff hand reaching out of the mud. Her breath would quicken, and those beautiful breasts would start bouncing as she called the man in question by every name except his own. From that point, Jean-Luc learned a very valuable lesson: *Angry women are so nice to look at.*

And now, what luck he had, there was Béatrice, the woman who had never showed him much of any reaction at all, suddenly fuming in the doorway, making those breasts rise and fall and rise and fall. O, blessed be the words that pushed her over the edge!

5

"Call you what?" Jean-Luc said calmly. The sun had come out.

Béatrice's chest tightened. *Speak, damn it, speak*, she said to herself, but nothing came. She closed her eyes.

"Are you okay, Béatrice?" Jean-Luc asked, unable to hide his smile. He was sure she was about to cry. Then he would be able to console her, maybe even give her a hug. Jean-Luc waited patiently, but when Béatrice's eyes opened, they were completely dry.

"*Miss Marilyn,*" Béatrice pronounced. She realized she had never said this name out loud herself. It sounded so sharp just then, she touched her neck as if she had been cut.

"Hey, I didn't mean it like…" Jean-Luc's smile began to deflate.

"Like *what…*?" she asked.

"Like…" He searched awkwardly for the right words. "Like…the way…everyone else means it… Listen, I didn't meant to upset you," he continued, "I just wanted to stop by and…you know…say hi."

"No," Béatrice said directly. She thought of the silent, floating shoe.

"Okay, listen. I'll let you go," Jean-Luc said. Béatrice continued to glare.

"See ya tonight…" he added meekly and crossed the street before she could respond.

6

Buh-bye big boy… A voice mists over from a long highway between Dresden and Prague.

Next time bring one of your white roses…. Another responds from a room with no windows.

At that very moment, somewhere years back, in Stuttgart, Germany, a ball of saliva lands on the inner thigh of a young girl whose hair is twisted into two thick chestnut braids. It slews down, leaving a moist trail on her pale, preteen skin, and drops onto the carpeted hallway. The owner of this saliva, a young man with a simple name, turns around and retucks his black, button-down shirt into faded black jeans.

XX
TELEPHONE

1

By the time César was back in the city from his audition, the light was already making way for evening. He bought a can of beer from the corner store and put the cold aluminium shell to his swollen nose. The shape of the can and the shape of his nose did not make good partners. César dabbed the dewy can, horizontally, diagonally, base then edge, unable to find a suitable fit. He finally gave in to holding the can under the base of his nose, cradling its weight against the bones in his face.

As he walked, the can rolled slightly and pressed into the bruising. César stopped, pulled his cell phone out of his pocket. No calls. He knew it was too soon for a call. But he could already hear Marcel's voice: *You really reeled it in there, they could not stop talking about you!*

César stuffed the phone back into his pocket. As he crossed the street, a woman holding the hand of her son stopped to look at him. César couldn't help but smile at them. The woman pulled her son to her hip.

2

When he got home he put the can of beer in the fridge. He looked at his face in the mirror. His under-eyes were puffy and rimmed with red. The sides of his nose were inflated, already yellowing with traces of violet. There was some dried blood on his nostrils and on the cleft above his lip. César's mother had said that it was that small valley below the nose where God left his fingerprint on each child at birth. Now God's fingertip had dried blood on it.

César couldn't help but feel slightly proud of his look. It was the closest he would get to looking like Julio César Chavez the boxer. César wished his brothers could see him now. But he let go of that thought, because it didn't matter in the end. The only person who needed to see him like this saw him. He was sure Manny would have called him *handsome.*

He thought of washing the dried blood off, but decided to leave it there. No hurry. He went to his computer and turned it on. He took out his cell phone and placed it near the keyboard. He pressed the light button, and the phone flashed to show him the time, but no calls. In all fairness, it really was too early to receive the call.

He went to the fridge and got out the can of beer, opened it, and took a swig. Why not celebrate? He went back to his desk and placed the can next to the cell phone. He checked the phone again, just in case he had left it on silent and a call came in between the moment he had set it down and the moment that he went to the fridge. The phone was fully charged, ready to ring, but showed, as before, no calls. He set it back down in its place and took a seat.

He logged into his email account. As the inbox was loading, César's eyes veered towards the phone. He resisted, keeping his fingers on the computer keyboard. The computer screen showed five new messages. The most recent, 70% off flights to Latin America. The next two, upcoming theater events. The fourth, an email from José inviting him to a show he was in. José was a friend he had made at acting school years back with whom he had kept in touch. José was from Guatemala, a dancer-actor, who was also dedicated to his art.

He was always inviting César to a show he was in, always in a small theater with a lonely name like the Theater of Two Dreams.

César couldn't quite call what he had with José a relationship, but they enjoyed each other's company for a while, went home together every now and then, even held hands at parties when drunk enough. But those days were long gone. José was now with a French guy, a mouse-eyed writer-director who was always telling funny rehearsal stories.

It embarrassed César to think about it, but José was the only guy he could refer to as an ex-boyfriend, except for Stefan. And Stefan he wished he could erase from his memory altogether.

Over the years César pulled away from the concept of "looking" altogether, and had resigned himself to being "married to his art." This statement freed him from the thought of having to experience all those frightening and stressful feelings that came with trying to be intimate with someone. He turned his energy inward, into the world of characters within him, filled with such interesting, beautiful, savage men, he often wished he could walk into their lives and never come back to his own.

He glanced back at his computer at the last email. The subject heading was: "Julio César, it's me." César inhaled to laugh then stopped because it shot a pain through his nose. Spam emails. They really take advantage; just when the excitement sparks that someone long forgotten has found you and somehow, yes, now they will confess something quite meaningful from your shared past—right then you find out that Dr. Forhernbäch is concerned about your hair loss, or that a balloon-breasted teen just got a webcam and would love to take this opportunity to chat with you. Just as César was about to delete the email, he noticed the sender address: gRaciasALAvIDa

Julio César, it's me.

3

From: gRaciasALAvIDa
Subject: Julio César, it's me

Julio César, it's me. The one who, from a distance, in my window, watched you and loved you.

I was young then, I was a virgin. So was my love.

Most people think I'm unlucky. (The things that happened to me.) LUCK is a dull thing. Like dice. It lands with a dumb grin, no matter the side. Should I have made a parade of my voice?

Should I have sung for my parents, for my husband, for you?

Should I have sung for the TV, for the radio, for the people of Mexico?

In life, I did not achieve a thing.

But, Julio César, there was a moment, in our youth, when I looked at you and my eyes reflected and came back to me as light. My whole being was illuminated. That was when my love became sharp.

When love is sharp it outlives the body. This is why I don't care much for LUCK.

So César, the actor, my European boy,

I could cut your throat with my love.

Gracais a la vida,

Rosa

4

César took his eyes off the screen and looked out to the window. No one. Rooftops. Dusk. The moon was showing itself like a bald spot upon the sky. He looked back at the computer screen. His eyes trailed across the words of Rosa's email like a stray dog.

When he was finished, he glanced back at his window. The nighttime air was turning marble. He turned back to his laptop and began rereading the email a third time. This time, the words rose to the surface through his own voice.

…*Gracias a la vida. Rosa.* César heard himself say.

As he finished the last word, his eyes went back to the window. He looked out at the night separated from him by the glass. Then his focus softened and he saw his own reflection. His eyes had dark smudges at the inner edges and his nose was puffed and bruised. *Handsome.* Inside his nostrils, a warmth grew and spread down, then blanketed that small valley above his lip where God touched him at birth. The warmth crawled slowly over the roof of his top lip, then with one quick jut slid down into his mouth like a child down a slide. He opened his mouth and caught the child with his tongue. Iron and lemon rind.

His nose was bleeding again.

5

César wiped the blood off with the back of his hand, then looked back at the computer screen. The words on the screen seemed to harden, like clenching teeth. He stood up and walked the couple of steps it took him to get to his small bathroom. He flicked on the bathroom light and looked into the mirror, tilting his head back. He saw another slew of blood coming at him, so he pulled some toilet paper off and stuffed it into his nose. This shot a pain through his sinuses and down his cheeks and into his gut. It made his stomach muscles flinch as if he would vomit.

César looked at his nose again close up. It looked like an over-ripe fruit. He reached his fingers up to touch the bone inside it. He knew this would give him an awful, mutilating feeling, but he wanted to experience it again. He pressed down firmly. His stomach contracted as he gagged immediately. His eyes teared up. He blinked and looked directly into the mirror.

"J'vai ti-tuay." *I'mana kill you* he said in French.

The phrase felt theatrical, inauthentic. He pressed down hard on his nose again. An acidic fog exploded in his throat and his eyes popped open. Instead of vomit, the words behind the phrase flew out, straight into his own reflection.

"TE MATO PUTA," he coughed up.

He spat into the sink and looked up again.

"TE MATO..."

He spat again, then wiped his mouth

TE MATO, **JOSE.**

He snorted. Blood misted his chin.

TE MATO, **RAUL.**

Blood misted the white sink.

TE MATO, **CHEKHOV.**

He spat. He grabbed the sides of the sink. He looked up and pulled close into the mirror.

"TE MATO, ***JULIO CÉSAR CHAVEZ!"*** he screamed.

TE MATO, **VIOLETA,** *TE MATO,* **ROSA,** *TE MATO,* **MAMA,** *TE MATO,* **TE MATO, TE MATO, CÉSAR EL ACTOR!**

6

Underneath his screaming, the music couldn't have been more beautiful. There, on the desk, next to his computer. His phone was ringing.

César leaped at the phone, grabbing it, dropping it, catching it, and answering it.

"H-h-he-llo?" he said, panting.

"Hello, hello."

"Marcel?"

"Where are you, César, can you hear me over there?"

"Yes I can hear you, I was just..."

"Great! Good to hear! César..."

"Yeah?"

"I was wondering if you—"

"I'm *your man!*" César said deeply, almost threatening.

"You are, you are…" said Marcel, and César smiled widely into the phone. "Listen, César, I know I'm your agent, but…" Marcel's voice turned a bit sheepish. "I consider you my buddy as well."

"Really? I mean. Me…too…"

"Oh César, that's great! That's really great to hear."

"No problem. So about— "

"Yes, exactly, that's exactly why I'm calling…"

The gilded finger of "Melody" is playing the sky like a harp.

"Do you have any plans tonight, César?"

"No nope nope totally free, do they need me to—"

"Actually, I was wondering if—"

"Yes, I can, I'm free!"

Violeta Parra's singing and smiling, singing and smiling.

"Oh, César I really appreciate this, I really do!"

"Sorry?"

"If you could pick up my daughter."

"Huh?"

"My daughter. She's coming in tonight. At the train station, Gare de l'Est."

"Oh."

Marcel gave César the details, time, place, train number, and César nodded solemnly and wrote the information down on a piece of paper. It was too late to take back his offer. Just before hanging up, Marcel added: "Also…if you wouldn't mind…taking her for a walk."

"Uh. Okay."

"Great!"

"So…what does your daughter look like?" César asked.

"Well…buddy…you remember the photos in my office?"

"Sure. I mean, which one?"

"Both!"

And with that, Marcel hung up. As César set down the phone down, it began to occur to him that this errand may well be part of the audition process. The more he thought about it, the more it seemed quite likely that it was in fact connected. He just had to play it smart. He zipped his jacket, grabbed his cell phone. He thought he could feel it about to ring, but it kept quiet. He stuffed it into his pocket and ran out the door.

7

There was a phone ringing somewhere else. The woolen man held the receiver up to the black wool over his cheek. It rang and rang. He stayed calm, sure that the person he was trying to reach would be there. And sure enough, the line was picked up.

"Hello…" Emmanuelle said.

"¿Cómo estás, preciosa?" The man's mouth moved behind the black wool.

"Who is this?" she said.

"Playin stoopid with me, princessa?"

The woolen man could feel the woman rolling her eyes at him. Then, by the difference in breath over the line, he heard her taking the phone away from her mouth and preparing to hang up on him. At this, an electric bolt went through his nerves.

"PUT THAT MOTHAFUCKIN PHONE BACK TO THAT SWEET SMOOTH EARLOBE, BITCH."

He heard the woman's breath quicken.

"Shh, calm down, bébé, I play nice wid you. So princessa, don speak no spanich, datz ok, I'm multilingual…mmm…I hear dat bébé heart of yers go boomboom lika bunny—dunbe scared o'me…"

In the pause, he could feel the woman pulling away.

"NATASHA, WHAT DID I SAY PUTA MADRE!" he shouted into the phone.

"Natasha is not my name," Emmanuelle replied.

"I'm juss playin wichou. Don't j'you like to play? If I waz overder I'd give you a kiss-kiss, mmm."

"*Don't come near me,*" Emmanuelle said.

"Hé stoopid, I'm far away on a phone talking to you. An no offens, bébé, but you aint da one I really wana see…"

"Who do you want?"

"Who you tink, stoopid. Manny wanna see *Miss Playboy.* Manny gotta real hard-on for Miss Playboy. Manny bout to bust his load juss tinkin bout it, shit. Manny wanna get his cum all over Miss Playboy, nice an creamy all up on dem big boobies, fuk man, Miss Playboy got Manny ready to xplode!"

"Stop calling her that," Emmanuelle said.

"Callin who wat," the man echoed.

"My sister."

"Yer sister. Yer sister. Dats real precious family shit. Id likta cork up yer troat wiff my dick, stik it all da way in, till u cant breathe, bitch."

"Well, you can't. You're far away talking on the phone, remember."

"Lissen to you, smartass bitch."

"Don't call me that either."

"Bébé gurl, I'm guna call you an yer sweetass sister whateverdafuck I want. I'm guna come by tonite and wen I look at you in da eyes, den you won be such a smartass bitch."

There was a pause as Emmanuelle took in the man's words.

"You lissenin OR WHAT?"

"*I'm listening,*" Emmanuelle said.

The woolen man pulled the black wool up to his nose, letting his bare lips touch the receiver. "*See you tonite,*" he said in one hot breath.

8

Emmanuelle's head flinched up from the pillow. She looked to the window. A blue glow was coming through the darkness. It was almost dawn.

Emmanuelle quietly peeled the covers open and crawled out of the bed. She rolled the covers back, looked at her sleeping sister for a moment, then tiptoed back to her room.

9

Years away, a ten-year-old girl with puffed eyes walks into her big sister's room.

I can't sleep, Bee.

Years away, a young bride is lying lifeless at the bottom of the bathtub.

Years away, a reporter asks a glazed-eyed boxer:

So how does it feel to be the world champion?

Years away, Violeta shoots herself in the head.

Years away, a man extends a fresh, white rose.

Years away, children sing the national anthem around a gagging girl.

I'm just a fighter... You are my country, you are my family.

My fists are yours.

A young girl's tailbone hits the edge of the stairs.

A sleek red door closes and the Mercedes drives off.

XXI

CIRCLE OF STONES

1

BÉATRICE AND THE GIRL she remembers not to call "Sabine" stand in the warm sand.

"Sit down, Béatrice," the girl tells her. "Not there, stupid. Right here."

Béatrice shifts her feet warily in the sand. "Here?" she asks.

The girl places her hand on Béatrice's shoulder and pushes her down.

"DUH."

After the stone circle is arranged, the girl flips the tail end of each of her braids behind her and says, "You ready?"

"...Yeah."

"Didn't your parents teach you any manners?"

"Huh?"

"Say *Yes ma'am* when you answer me."

"Yes...ma'am."

The girl looks down at the stone circle and takes her time turning each stone clockwise, counter-clockwise, as if cracking a code. She speaks as she turns.

"Béatrice, you're pretty."

"Thanks."

"Pretty girls grow up to be happy and stupid in the face."

"Oh."

"Oh??"

"Yes ma'am."

"Don't *yes ma'am* me on that, I know I'm right, I don't need your approval."

Béatrice bites her lip.

"My mom says I'm *the most beautiful girl in the world*...but she's stupid. I'm okay for now, but I don't see things going uphill for me in the future in the way of looks. Which is, by the way, what is called *a blessing in disguise*. It means I don't have to worry about turning out happy and stupid in the face (YUK!). I'd rather be sad than happy that's for sure! There's *nothing, nothing, nothing* worse in this whole wide world than being STUPID, got it?"

"Yes ma'am."

"That's why I pity you, Béatrice. You are very un-for-tu-nate."

"I am?"

"Yes, that's what I just said! See, it's already kicking in. Your stupidity."

Béatrice touches her face around the edges and feels for vibrations changing beneath her skin.

2

"WELL, YOU WANNA KNOW WHAT I SEE? DO YOU? Hold my ankles tighter, Béatrice! WELL? I'm gunna slip, stupid! READY? You holding? READY? My ankles, Béatrice! READY? I'm gunna fall in! READY TO KNOW YOUR FUTURE, BÉATRICE?"

"Tell me," a woman's voice says from Béatrice's childish mouth.

"I see you with ENORMOUS boobs and you're walking around with your shoulders BACK and you're swaying LEFT, RIGHT showing off your rack. And you're jingling a pair of keys. To a house that doesn't have any windows. It's a tall, tall tower, actually. You're inside a tall, tall tower. You're at the top. You're not even wearing a shirt or a bra. You're just sitting there, showing off your big boobies, hoping someone'll look up. You think you're sitting by the window and people can see you, but there are no windows, stupid! And you're jingling your keys for music, 'cause you're so lonely for someone to see your boobies. You think you're some sort of *PRINCESS*. But you're just a—a—a prin-pin-pes—piz—*PIZDA* in a tower.

"HA HA HA

"HA HA HA

HA HA—"

The girl falls forward and her laughter is quickly stubbed out by the sand. The grains muffle her voice and soak up the flow of blood from her nose.

XXII

LA SANGRE LLAMA

1

CÉSAR WAITED ON THE platform at Gare de l'Est for the TGV 9554 from Stuttgart to come in. Sweaty and chilled by the breeze from the constant flow of people rolling their suitcases left and right, his heart was still racing from the run over. He should have taken the metro, but public transportation makes him anxious when he is on his way to an unfamiliar meeting. In these cases, he prefers to walk, and of course walking, when he's anxious, always turns into a run.

He looked at the ivory-faced clock with large black roman numerals. He saw two arrows crossing paths at a molecularly slow rate. He concentrated on the arrows, but still had no idea what time it was. He pulled out his cell phone and read the numbers. It was 6:38 and the train was due in at 7:01. He had time.

Since he only had the bare information about this meeting, his brain used the waiting time to review and regroup:

1. Marcel has a daughter
2. Correction, Marcel has two daughters
3. Correction, Marcel has two photos of young girls on his shelves
4. Side thought, I hope those photos are of his daughters
5. Continued side thought, Marcel's not a pervert, is he?

6. Resolution to side thought, No, Marcel is a nice guy who only keeps photos of young women if they are his daughters
7. Back on track, Marcel's daughter needs to be picked up and taken on a walk
8. Info, she's coming in from Stuttgart at 7:01
9. Fact, Stuttgart is in Germany
10. Side thought, the last time I was in Germany was two years ago
11. Side thought blossoming into memory: Stefan.

2

Back in Mexico, when César realized that the feelings he had for his male classmates were not spoken of by others, nor written about in books, nor portrayed in films, nor sung in songs, he was both frightened and mesmerised by his secret. As he grew up, he understood very clearly that there would be serious consequences to any expression of this secret. He had to keep the cover on it tight and remain likeable. On the other hand, the desires he buried deeper and deeper became ever more more mysterious and seductive. Once he embraced this inter-frequency existence, he discovered a whole world, hidden from the obvious eye, where men desired men deeply, wholly, desperately, in books, in films, in songs, and all around him. Of course, the trick was that everything had to stay between the lines.

3

When he moved to Paris, he was shocked by the blatantness of homosexual life. It seemed to him quite vulgar to see a man openly kiss another man on the mouth, in broad daylight. What about all those films he'd watched, where all men could do was eye each other and drink together, with that vigorous, muffled yearning tugging between them? What happened to the magnetic silence, the alluring space between bodies, the unspoken arousal?

In his acting school he kissed his first man, José. Of course he tried to pretend like it wasn't his first. How embarrassing it would have been for José to find out that César was nearing his mid-twenties and had never touched his lips to another man's, let alone held a penis in his mouth or swallowed another man's sperm.

César proceeded to shadow José's movements, careful not to let it show that he was learning. Every intimate interaction was stalked with the faint terror of being found out to be a virgin. Just when César found himself letting go and getting used to certain intimate acts, José told him that he didn't think things were really working out between them, but hoped they could still be friends. César had quickly said, *Of course, sure, no problem*, then spent a week avoiding eye contact with José and crying in the evenings.

4

After a while the urge to try it out with someone else grew. That's when he tried a couple of gay bars, but found himself repulsed by his surroundings, flinching at the touch of other men. So he retreated to a more familiar terrain, between the lines; he signed up on an internet dating site. That's where he met Stefan.

5

Stefan lived in Dresden, where he worked in a lab as a researcher. In his profile photos, he had an athletic jaw and considerate eyes, blue as boyhood, over which sat a pair of simple thin-framed glasses, purely functional. When they finally spoke on Skype, César was mesmerised with the way Stefan pressed his full lips together and made his jawline flex when he paused to think, and how he would continuously push back his fine blond hair with his palm.

Stefan reminded him of an actor in an old movie, a hero in a Western perhaps. He tried to remember the film's name or the actor's name, but could never pinpoint it, and so Stefan's face lingered in the timeless desert where the land was quiet, handsome, and tearless.

And yet, this beautiful creature was like him. He didn't go out much, especially not in the gay scene, partly because he had social anxiety (as he explained) and also because he was always working at the lab. The two quickly bonded over their introverted particularities and their strong willingness to invest in the idea of romance.

For months, they continued to chat over Skype, César, enchanted with the way Stefan's cheeks flushed with red patches when he got stuck on a sentence he couldn't finish, the way his hand opened and closed as he spoke, then pulled back over his hair. Those were the most deeply joyful months of César's life.

6

"Blut ist dicker als Wasser," Stefan would say slowly then wait for César to laugh. César laughed with him, even though he did not understand the reference. Stefan repeated the phrase, in English, "Blood is thicker than water." He was, of course, referring to his research, not to any particular familial loyalty.

"Biological ties are no better or worse than conditioning when all is said and done. It's just two different kinds of elastic, if you think about it. Biology is a much thicker elastic, I mean pulling even a centimeter of leeway is a life's work!"

Stefan pulled gently on his own earlobe. "Evolution," he said and chuckled.

César smiled hesitantly, lowering his gaze. When he looked back up again, he saw Stefan watching him intently.

"La sangre llama," César said.

Stefan raised an eyebrow.

"In Spanish we have that expression too. But we say *la sangre llama.*"

"And what does it mean?" Stefan asked flirtatiously.

"'Blood's calling,'" César replied.

That's when both of them agreed to meet for the first time in real life.

7

They decided on Stuttgart as a halfway meeting point between both of them. They rented a hotel near the train station.

When they spotted each other in the Arrivals Hall, they both looked away shyly, then walked towards each other solemnly, like a bride and groom. Face to face, they had forgotten all customs. Stefan extended his hand as César lunged in for a kiss. Stefan's knuckle jabbed into César's gut and César pecked him on the cheek.

Outside the building, Stefan pointed up to the inscription: *daß diese Furcht zu irren schon der Irrtum selbst ist. G.W.F.H.* He explained it was Hegel. "…That this fear of making a mistake is a mistake itself." César looked into Stefan's eyes then, and thought *I am ready for love.*

8

They checked into their hotel, César giddy with the idea that the clerk could never imagine what they would do together in their room.

In the room, with the door closed, Stefan opened the sliding closet door and put his bag there. César put his near the small garbage bin beneath the desk. The two men approached each other nervously. Stefan blushed and smiled. César looked down then back up then couldn't help but smile as well. The two leaned in and their lips met.

9

The kiss was gentle, yet made César feel all the more anxious. He sped up his lips and hardened his tongue, looking for something he couldn't name. He felt Stefan's mouth, his tongue, his teeth, no matter what he touched, it all felt like dull matter. Stefan, feeling César's racing heart through his mouth, wrapped his arms around César and pulled him into his chest. When their bodies met, César expected Stefan to rip his shirt off or thrust his pants down, but instead Stefan just held him there, tightly, warmly. César's breath was shallow. He could feel the panic rising into his head. *What is Stefan doing? Why is he holding me in this void?*

César blurted out, "Hit me."

Stefan let go of César and ran his hand through his hair. "What?"

"Smack me around," César replied.

Stefan just stood blankly in front of César, his arms hanging limp. At that moment César realized that even with Stefan right in front of him, he was unbearably lonely. And his loneliness was quite ordinary. It had nothing to do with Hollywood heroes, but was as vulgar as a panting porn actor's.

César squeezed his fist and punched Stefan square on his beautiful jaw.

10

Stefan grabbed his face and folded over on to the floor. He looked up at César through his fingers with wild, disgusted eyes.

"*WHAT* is *wrong* with you!" Stefan demanded.

César stumbled back, stuttering "...*ll..lll...llaa...*"

"WHAT WHAT WHAT?" Stefan spoke with a hard voice.

All César could think was that he should have been one of his tough characters with Stefan from the start, instead of being himself. His anger could have been handsome, masculine, romantic. Instead it was just crippled and perverse, an excuse for the absence of love.

Stefan was back on his feet, his shoulders wide and his neck muscular and straight. He took a step towards César.

"*ll...lll...llaa...*" César continued to stutter.

"WHAT IS IT?" Stefan repeated.

"*La sangre llama,*" César said, then flinched at his own voice.

On the train back to Paris, in the small, steel bathroom, César leaned his hot forehead against the metal and cried.

11

At Gare de l'Est, César clenched his jaw and pushed these fragments away, back into the shadows of his mind. He looked at the clock again and it now appeared that the long arrow was winning. Then he heard the gush of steam and the screech of metal wheels on iron. The train had come in. The doors slid open. Passengers started to step off and fill up the platform.

He watched the people exit. He looked carefully at every female who descended, from preteens (who knows how young she was) to mid-thirties (who knows how old those photos were). He observed young girls with backpacks, women with briefcases, ladies with neck scarves, teens in tight jeans, older women in flat shoes and stockings, younger ones in platform shoes, girls who wore no makeup, others with glossy lips and clumped eyelashes. César had begun to forget what he was looking for in the first place.

He called back the image of the photos on Marcel's shelves. Thick chestnut hair. Childish nose, freckles. A slight smirk beneath those expressionless lips. No one seemed to fit this composite.

12

A nerve pinched in his foot. He looked down. There was a head of chestnut hair. A woman looked intently up at him. Her hair was pulled back tightly and clipped with a simple clasp.

At first glance, you could mistake her for a girl. The childlike nose with the freckles. But there were tiny folds at the corners of her eyes, just behind her small oval glasses. This was a woman, maybe thirty years old.

"You're César the actor, I presume."

Her hands were folded over a small blue leather purse on her knees. She was in a wheelchair. "I'm Sabine."

The woman raised one hand from her small blue leather purse and extended it towards César. "But I prefer you don't call me by this name."

César hunched down and shook her hand lightly, then released it. His arm felt dazed. He tried to get hold of himself, but the sight of the wheelchair made him uneasy. His lips tightened instinctively, afraid of what may come out.

"…What…should I…call you…?" César asked hesitantly.

Sabine's lips became firm. "Not *Sabine*," she said.

13

"Sorry to keep you waiting," Sabine continued frankly.

César winced a quick smile to let her know it was okay. In any case, she was basically on time, a few minutes here or there. He waited for her to say something else, but she didn't. César looked down at his shoe. It had a small black smear where the wheelchair had run into it. He looked back up at Sabine. Her lips were flat and her eyes were alert. They caught each other's glance by accident, and Sabine spoke: "When I was in Victoria, in Australia, four and half years ago, during the summer, all the trains had to be slowed down to 90 kph instead of 160kph, as the heat—which was particularly extreme that summer—expands the tracks and threatens derailment of trains traveling at the normal regulatory speed."

"Oh," César replied.

"Stuttgart is 622.4 kilometres from Paris."

"Oh…"

"I assume it's not optimal for you to spend your Friday evening picking up a woman in a wheelchair."

"Oh. Uh—no, no, it's great! I mean not *great* but it's…nice—*very nice.*"

"Anyway, I'll talk to Marcel and tell him you showed up. That way you can get what you need, is that correct?"

"That's what I thought, but—" César blurted out.

Sabine frowned.

"I mean…I dunno," César said meekly.

He was trying so hard not to stare at her two dead legs positioned neatly next to each other, he began to sweat again.

"Uh, your father—Marcel—told me to…" César spoke hesitantly.

"Yes?" Sabine looked up.

"Well, he told me to…" César didn't want to say it.

"Yes, Marcel told you to…?" Sabine inquired.

"Um."

César moved his lips around as if he had to sneeze. He was trying to buy time. Maybe she'd say it for him. Sabine waited patiently as César squirmed.

"Yes, I'm listening. Marcel told you to…?"

"To…uh…well…he…told me…to take you…*for a walk.*" César's eyes dropped down to Sabine's folded legs.

"Marcel told you to take *me* for a *walk*?"

César looked instantly away, unable to face Sabine's eyes.

"Yeah…"

César waited for Sabine to respond but she remained nailed-still. His eyes skimmed the floor and found a stepped-on cigarette butt encrusted in a crack. He shuffled his hands in his pockets and followed the crack with his eyes. What would this woman do? Would she scream at him? No, she didn't seem like the type. Would she scold him for his choice of words? More probable. Would she huff at his ignorance and run off? (Surely not run, she was in a wheelchair.) César blushed privately at this thought.

Sabine spoke up in a strong, definite tone. "Come on then. Take me for a walk."

14

César maneuvered the wheelchair around the crowded train station towards the exit. It was not as easy as he assumed it would be. The route to the main entrance became a series of starts and stops, spotted with points of panic as he avoided oncomers, trying to get the chair back under control so Sabine's lifeless knees would not knock a child's teeth out.

Sabine did not flinch once. She sat upright and poised, her torso like a plastic mannequin fixed to the chair. When César finally managed to get out of the train station, she spoke. "Let's go down to the canal."

César did not have much choice. He said "Okay" and sighed as he pushed the wheelchair over the brick-lined road.

15

People are a lot heavier sitting down, even if they have wheels attached. César struggled forward, but every couple of minutes had to jolt out of the way of a stranger who saw César clearly, but happened to miss Sabine, just below.

As they approached the canal, he started up the flat cement road which ran alongside the cafés. But Sabine asked to be closer to the water, so he was obliged to cross the street and join the cobblestone passageway. The wheelchair grumbled over the stones.

Along the edge of the canal, young people sat with bottles of wine or cans of beer at their feet; an open bag of chips, half indented like a couch cushion. Some had a proletarian-style picnic: bread, cheese, meat. In these groups, the guys wore loose long-sleeve shirts in earth-tone colors. Their fingers rolled cigarettes and their eyes gazed in intervals, at their friends and at these wondrous people called strangers.

Other groups were young people who were newly initiated into the job market, which was deflated except for the ever-booming sectors dealing with consumer appetites: advertising, marketing, business. They wore high-quality fabrics, cut and sewed together to both integrate and rebel against the fashion status quo. They pecked at green olives in plastic containers, slices of chorizo or salami, and broke up pieces of bread from baguettes; a container of oily grated carrots was open but untouched. A guy shuffled chips from the tube of Pringles and crunched them mechanically, unaffected by their taste. Then, of course, there was the discreetly luxurious group with their apéro-hour picnic, coal-black bottles of Freixenet Spanish Cava, biological cider, parmesan crackers, grain and seed crackers, rice crackers, hummus, eggplant dip, and multiple containers of strawberries (*Oh, look at that, you also brought strawberries!*). These were Scandinavians who had at some point "lived in London," Anglophones who were at some point "from New York," musicians just arrived from Germany or Japan and other artists from more exotic countries: Russia, Turkey, Iran.

A mixed group of Spanish and Italians spoke and ate and drank and listened to each other very loudly. They brought tupperwares of tapas and tall cans of cheap beer.

These groups of young people glanced casually at César and Sabine as they passed. Some remarked with hushed words. Some pointed at them with their chins. Others just looked away. César couldn't tell if it was his swollen nose or Sabine's dead legs that drew the attention.

César gripped each handle of the wheelchair and pushed her forward. He was grateful he couldn't see Sabine's face and that she couldn't see his. An agitation rumbled within him. Why did this woman have to make him parade with her like this, in front of all these people, all these young people, so well-adapted and unbothered by themselves?

Relájese, César, relax… he heard a gritty man's voice say to him in his head.

Diz is juss a test. Diz is onlee a test, mi amor.

16

"Closer," Sabine said.

They had found a free spot near the canal's edge. César pulled the wheelchair up to the barrier.

"Closer."

César wasn't sure if he could get any closer, but he rolled the chair forward a couple of inches until the front of the wheels dubbed against the barrier, and Sabine's dead legs swayed a couple of times from the impact.

Sabine sat very still. Since he could not see her face, he had no idea what sort of experience she was having in front of the water. Was she bored? Annoyed with him? Most importantly, was she reconsidering what she would report back to Marcel?

"Napoleon ordered the creation of this artificial waterway," Sabine began, "to provide the people of Paris with fresh water, which of course was a polite way to cut down on diseases such as dysentery and cholera amongst his swelling population. The year was 1802, to be exact. Not long after the first leopard was exhibited in America. Boston, to be exact. February second, to be exact. Admission was twenty-five cents."

César bracketed his eyebrows. "Oh."

"It obviously took a considerable amount of time to build the canal. But once it was in place, it was used as a transportation route, and so factories and warehouses were constructed along the quais. But, of course, times change, the world turns, the earth rotates— once every twenty-four hours from the point of view of the sun to be exact, and of course once every twenty-three hours, 56 minutes and 4 seconds from the point of view of the stars. One can look at it this way: a sticky-faced child makes a wish, and by the time the wish is in orbit, there's another sticky-faced child making a wish. And so on. Until the sky is full of unsatisfied orbiting wishes, like swarms of buzzing mosquitoes. Skinny, flimsy, dry-mouthed mosquitoes. They land on our skin and with their shaky lips they try to suck some life out, but of course they are too weak and it only gives the surface a slight tickling sensation and they can't reach the source. However, there are swarms of these wobbly-lipped wishes, and one day the next sticky-faced child turns to his mother and says, *Mama, the world is spinning too fast, I think I'm gunna be sick*, and of course before his *Mama* has time, he's already vomiting on her shoes."

César was at a loss. He did not even have a nonverbal sound to give as a response. He nodded in silence.

"What I am leading to, of course, is that by the mid-twentieth century, boat traffic was not as popular as it once was, so this canal was almost turned into a highway for efficiency's sake. It was a de-bate. In 1960—60—60—in 1960—"

"Very nice," César cut her off. He didn't mean to, but her speech was making him anxious again.

She fell silent. Her silence had a strong taste to it. Bitter and grainy, like the shell of a walnut.

"César the actor," Sabine said in a level tone. "Come and sit next to me, please."

César did as he was told.

First he squatted, but did not find this position comfortable. He contemplated sitting on the ground, but then he would be too low, at the level of her wheels. Then he looked in front of him—of course—he took a seat on the metal barrier.

Sabine turned her head and looked directly at César. She had smooth, well-kept skin which held a childhood freshness, and light freckles across her nose—that nose that still seemed to belong to a little girl. Yet, there was something very frightening about her, in the way she looked at him.

"So then. What happened to your nose?" Sabine asked. "Did you get in a fight?"

César gave her question some thought. "Um. Sort of," he replied.

Sabine looked at him for another long moment, then turned her head back towards the water and fell into her own thoughts. Then, keeping her eyes on the water, she spoke again: "Did you win?"

César's eyes perked up. *Depends. Depends on Marcel,* he wanted to say.

"...Don't know yet," César replied with a half smile.

XXIII
SWEET & HEAVENLY

1

Béatrice's father drove. Her mother was in the front. Her sister sat in the back, with Jean-Luc at her side, chivalrously taking the middle seat. He pressed into Emmanuelle when the car took a left, and into Béatrice when the car took a right.

In the car, Béatrice could smell something unmistakable. She knew exactly what it was: long-stemmed Stargazer lilies, split-open fuchsia stars rimmed with white, each petal freckled; in the bouquet were probably a couple of eucalyptus stems, and one or two lemon leaves.

When Béatrice was young she begged her mom for a cat. Her mother smiled and said to little Béatrice that she would get her a cat, but Stargazer lilies (one of her favorites) are highly toxic to cats, and she could not live without Stargazer lilies whereas she could live without a cat. Each time she brought them home her mother would bring the bouquet to Béatrice's face, saying, "Oh, just smell them, Béatrice, don't they smell sweet and heavenly?" In a matter of minutes, Béatrice would always have a migraine. She hoped heaven did not smell like this.

Over the years, she had tried again and again to express to her mother that she did not enjoy this scent. But every attempt to communicate this left her mother with the impression that Stargazer lilies were Béatrice's favorite flower.

The mother looked back at her from the front car seat.

"Oops, how'd you guess! I put them on my lap with a scarf over, so you wouldn't see it until after the concert. Oh well. Surprise…!"

She pulled the bouquet out from beneath the scarf and pushed it into Béatrice's face. Béatrice could already feel the particles gather in her throat. Her stomach swayed with a light nausea and her gut flinched.

"Sweet and heavenly," the father said and made a right turn.

As the car pivoted, Jean-Luc was pressed into Béatrice's shoulder.

"…Just like you," Jean-Luc whispered.

XXIV

KARL

1

César could not endure Sabine's silence just as he couldn't quite handle her small talk. Luckily, *God bless this machine,* the phone rang. Sabine unzipped the small purse on her lap and took out the phone. "Allo. Ich bin in Paris. ...Nein... Leite es an Christophe weiter. ...Ya...Tuesday, not Wednesday. Surtout pas, je vous avais expliqué. Okay, tak mi zavolej ...Oui...Oui...Okay, goodbye."

"Something important?" César asked.

"Work."

Sabine explained that she worked for the Volkswagen Group in Dresden as an engineer of some sort. (César almost blurted out, *I knew a guy from Dresden once,* but he stopped himself in time.) She mentioned computer modeling software and anticipating component behaviour and monitoring associated engineering issues with the final product, but all César could picture were those test cars with the dummies strapped inside that they crash into walls.

"Interesting stuff," César said.

Sabine continued to explain that the Volkswagen Group had partnered up with the Czech Republic's largest car manufacturer, Skoda Auto. That's why she took regular trips to Mlada Bleslav in the north of Prague to visit the giant Skoda manufacturing plant.

"The year of the big partnership was 1991, to be exact. I was barely twelve at the time, living in France. I didn't know a thing about the East and the West. The world map consisted of Paris, Bordeaux where my grandparents lived, the Aquitaine region where we spent our summers, Arcachon, Sanguinet Andernos-les-Bains, Dune du Pyla. But in 1991, as I'm sure you're aware, the Soviet Union fell, and thousands of newly made businessmen carried off the crumbs in a hurry. Some built empires. Some were greedy and took a piece too big and got crushed underneath."

Across the canal, a couple laughed together. Then their voices subsided.

"Only a year later, my mom moved me to Stuttgart and I got a taste of the changing world."

Sabine's mother, Marcel's ex-wife, met and married a German man from Stuttgart and moved there with Sabine when she was thirteen. Her mother's new husband brought with him a son from his previous marriage, Karl. Karl was seventeen, with a greasy blond shag of hair and a patch of fine hairs on his upper lip, but otherwise no facial hair. His cheeks darted out of his gaunt face, and his lips were heart-shaped. He was tall and bony. It did not help that he wore baggy blue jeans which he fastened to his skinny body with a flat, black leather belt slung tightly in the loops. Over his lean torso, he wore the usual white undershirt, and a short-sleeve, faded black button-up shirt (he buttoned every button, up to his protruding Adam's apple).

Most of the time, Karl just wanted to be left alone. So he was not thrilled to have two more people in his space to pester him. And if there was one thing Sabine was a natural in, it was pestering.

She asked Karl if he knew that Stuttgart, which was also known as Benztown, was where the automobile and the motorcycle were invented, by a certain Karl Benz. She wanted to know if Karl had been named after the inventor.

"No," Karl replied.

She continued then to inform Karl that the automobile and motorcycle were later industrialized by Gottlieb Daimler and Wilhelm Maybach (in 1887, to be exact) at the Daimler Motoren Gesellschaft (to be exact), and that she preferred the name Gottlieb or Wilhelm to Karl because to her "Karl sounds like someone who lacks ambition."

Karl scratched his chin, then left the room.

2

At first Karl spent most of his time in his room, on his computer. But after starting a new high school in Stuttgart, a beat-up car began turning up with four guys in it. It would honk on arrival and Karl would tuck his faded black shirt into his jeans and head out the door.

Karl's father and Sabine's mother, who were both worried about Karl's transition to the new family and the new school, were somewhat relieved to see he had found a group of friends. The only problem was that Karl still kept to himself, and never talked about his social life to them. As soon as he got in that car, though, the boys slapped each other's shoulders in such brotherhood that you could see Karl's eyes shine like two sunlit rivers.

"So…What do you do…with your friends, you watch movies, or you stay inside and play your games…?" Sabine's mother asked delicately.

Karl snorted. "Why would we waste our time on that?"

Karl's father interjected. "But you used to love your games. I mean, the ones with the cards and the ones online?"

"Not anymore."

Karl left more and more regularly in that old car with the boys. When Sabine's mother demanded to know where it was he was going, Karl said, "None of your business." When she demanded that he speak to her with respect, Karl said, "Earn it first." When Karl's father stepped in to reprimand the boy, Karl said, "Save it for your other illegit kid." With that, he slammed the door and was off to one of his *meetings*.

At least Karl had grown out of his introverted internet games and found some intrapersonal social activity, his father reasoned. This, like his games, was surely another adolescent phase. Both parents decided to leave it at that and wait for Karl to outgrow this phase independently.

3

A month before graduation, Karl had managed to grow a thin, golden goatee on his chin. He had also shaved his head. Then, coming home in the middle of dinner, he announced that he was moving out. His father set his fork and knife down and stood up.

"Karl. You come and go without a word. You've no manners with your mother and sister—"

"You mean your new whore and her little bitch," Karl said flatly.

The father squared up to his son. He was twice as bulky as the boy, but his son's eyes were packed with more muscle. The men looked at each other in silence.

Sabine waited for the father to hit his son in the face. But this was not a man who could use his strength for violence. Anger surged through his body limply, like tears running down his veins. The father peered into Karl's eyes, trying to find his son. Everything was familiar, except what lived within those two holes. Karl broke the eye contact and glanced at Sabine.

"Karl. Look at me," demanded his father. "I raised you to be a man of respect and principle."

"I am, *Father*."

Karl took a seat and began to speak about integrity.

4

Sabine and her mother were asked to leave the room. Karl's voice was heavy with concern and responsibility as he spoke to his father, about human suffering. He explained ugliness so precisely that one could imagine he was performing surgery on the bellies of ants. His father was ready to let the past go, to reach out to his son and take him into his arms and help him believe in his own beauty, when Karl suddenly said, "…Ugliness, like *yours*."

His father sat still, taking apart this phrase in his head.

Karl picked up where he left off without changing expression. Now, however, the content of his speech jarred more and more with his calm, charitable tone. He spoke highly of an older woman, for whom his father almost assumed he had romantic feelings, until Karl quoted her speech to young German women, urging them to lead a lifestyle that minimizes the risk of rape in order to avoid the mutilation of human life. He explained to his father the Sabbath of perverts, when men degrade themselves with other men. He asked if his father had ever put a cockroach in his mouth. At this, his father almost jumped from his seat. He continued, "How, then, could he kiss *that woman* on the lips day after day?" By that woman, of course, he meant Sabine's mother.

It was clear now. Perhaps it had been clear from the moment Karl got in the car with the boys, from the moment he began tucking in his shirt, from the moment he shaved his head, but now it was undeniably clear, and yet his father was desperate to make it less clear.

"Why would you say such a thing?" Karl's father pleaded.

"I say it because others remain cowering in their silence. In their silence, their tongues, like yours, *father*, are covered with the filth of it all. With the filth of the ugliness around us, *father*. The filth on the flailing tongue of this country, *father*. The filth in the crevices of this decaying world. The filth you, *father*, have brought into our own house. And the filth you have dug your manhood into, you reek *FATHER* you smell of IT!"

5

Karl moved out and despite his father's continual efforts, cut ties with the family. By then, Sabine had entered high school. She did not have many friends, partly because of her relentless commentary on everything. She informed everyone around her, her teachers included, of all kinds of facts that they surely should know, unless of course they were downright stupid. She retreated into her studies and did exceedingly well. But she remained a girl who was hard to like.

The more time that passed without Karl in the family, the more his father believed that it was not Karl who had abandoned the family, but rather he who had abandoned Karl. His father lay next to his new wife at night, with a disgusting texture growing in his mouth. If Sabine's mother tried to reach over to him, he would flinch, then say he was sorry, then get up and go to the hallway to look at a childhood photo of his son. Karl, barely standing on the grass, with his biological mother behind, holding him up. Now both this woman and the son were gone. The thought terrorized him: *It's all my fault.*

6

What the father did not know was that Karl made regular visits back in his absence, to rifle through the apartment and stock up on supplies. He would come home wearing the same loose black jeans with a black shirt tucked in, except this time with black gloves. He carefully went through the drawers in each room and slipped valuables into his pockets: cash, jewelry, the occasional credit card.

Sabine was the only one who knew, because she had caught him once.

7

"That's my mother's," Sabine said from the hallway, referring to her mother's wedding ring from her first marriage. Karl put a leather-gloved finger to his mouth as he slipped the ring out of its case and down his long jean pocket.

"You can't take that. It's not yours. That's stealing. You're a thief. You're disrupting society. You belong in prison." Sabine spoke in an endless trail as Karl tried to move past her. After several attempts, Karl saw this girl would not budge from the doorway. He leaned down and looked his stepsister straight in the eyes and said, "*Sabine.*" As he reached out to take her shoulders, Sabine began to flail her small hands at Karl's chest, screaming, "DON'T CALL ME THAT, DON'T CALL ME THAT!"

Sabine charged at him, but Karl flung his long arms out and pushed her back. She fell into the wall, but got up immediately and charged at him again. He caught her at her shoulders, then grabbed her throat to stop her screaming. He brought his face into her bulging eyes.

"Sa…bine," he said. His hot breath went into her nose.

Sabine twisted and heaved.

"SA-BINE," he repeated. "SABINE. SABINE. SABINE."

Tears and mucus ran down her face. Karl let go and Sabine stumbled back coughing. She caught her breath and glared at Karl. Her eyes terrified him. When she charged at him again, he pushed her back with greater violence than before. She ricocheted straight into the hallway table, then dropped onto the floor. Her skirt flew up to her waist and her chin tucked into her collarbone. Karl looked at her immobile body, at her barely teenage legs and her thin, white underwear the texture of gauze. He gritted his teeth, made a ball of saliva in his mouth, and then spat it out onto her naked thigh.

8

When Sabine came to, it was already late afternoon. She got up, fixed her skirt, and wandered dazed down the stairs.

That evening, when her stepfather asked what had happened to her head, she said she did not remember. When her mother came into her room at bedtime and kneeled at her bedside and told her to be honest now, Sabine said, "I'm always being honest."

9

Years later, after achieving a high-level university degree, Sabine had moved to Dresden, got a well-paying job at the automobile manufacturing company where she had authority and integrity, and finally a position where she was paid to boss people around and inform them of things they should know.

The thing that continued to bother her were the sightings. She could never be sure, but she had the impression that perhaps Karl was following her.

She first spotted someone who looked like Karl at a café near her apartment building. Then she swore she had spotted him again, behind a tree in the small park across the street from where she was having dinner by herself at a Turkish restaurant.

The years passed and she accumulated many sightings of Karl. She had changed the lock on her door a total of nine times in three years. But Karl, whether he was there or not, never came face to face with her. Maybe she had imagined him. Every time she called home, her mother and stepfather each swore that they hadn't seen or heard from Karl since the night he had left. Though her mother once told her in secret that she thought she had seen his face on TV during the riots in Leipzig. Then again, she couldn't be sure. "Oh, honey, they all look the same with their arm stretched out into the air like a bunch of idiots. Your grandfather would turn in his grave if he knew. It was one thing for me to marry your father—"

"Which one?" Sabine cut off her mother.

"Oh, darling, don't hate me, please don't hate me."

After a silence on the phone, Sabine pronounced in a childish voice, "I don't care anymore."

After she hung up the phone, she remembered her grandpa telling her about his time in the concentration camp at Drancy, just outside of Paris, before he was deported, how some stole bread from children and others died for strangers. He had believed that heroism would be a greater force than organized cruelty. Perhaps his belief system was his saving grace, as he survived. At the end of his stories, however, his tone would drop as he said, "…Look around. What a world to survive for…"

Sabine went to the bathroom mirror and slapped herself hard in the face.

10

In her wheelchair now, on the canal with César, she expressed none of this. It passed unspoken beneath her rolling list of facts and figures of Dresden, automobiles, highways, and emperors. He waited patiently for the pauses to say "uh huh" and "oh" as if he were filling in mortar between bricks.

Then she closed her lips, as if for good. The sudden silence concerned César.

"S-s-so…you'ah…miss your family?"

Sabine turned to look at César. There was a flash in her eyes.

"Come on. We aren't done with our walk."

César got up, brushed the back of his jeans. He looked around him at the young people, drinking, smoking, snacking, belonging to their moments. He sighed and pulled the wheelchair around, back onto the cobblestone road.

11

"Here, right here, you missed it," Sabine said.

César made a brisk U-turn with the wheelchair. He was getting the hang of this.

"Here?" he asked.

"Yes, here."

The terrace of the bar was crowded with smokers and chatterers. César wheeled up, excused them, and tried to get in. People were quickly annoyed by César's attempt at entry, but as soon as they saw the woman in the wheelchair, they would quickly smile and scoot themselves in the most polite manner. Body by body, the crowd opened up and César inched Sabine toward the entrance.

Around the edge of the door, behind the sitting drinkers, were rows of standing ones, with their backs to César making an impenetrable comb-tooth wall. César reached over and tried to tap some people on the shoulder. One person turned, then another, then a small passageway was made and bodies shifted to the side like a curtain being drawn.

César placed his hands on the wheelchair handles and gave Sabine a soft slide forward. A light reflecting from the stage blinded him momentarily, then shifted over his head. In front of him, all the tables were full with people sitting, sipping their beers and wines and looking intently at the stage.

On the stage, a bearded man held a double bass and strummed. On the other side, a clean-shaven man played the piano. Behind them, a bald drummer held the rhythm steady. At the center, in a long, black lace gown, the woman held a note with her eyes closed. Just as the note finished, she opened her eyes and looked at the crowd. Her hand let go of the microphone and swept over the lobe of her ear, then up over her tightly wound, blonde chignon.

XXV

THE WHITE ROSE

1

The light from the terrace of the bar spilled into the quiet street, where it lit the fingers and mouths of the crowd. Across the road, a solemn stone church had its back to the lively bodies on the terrace. Young men chatted with young women with their hips crooked forward into their drinks. Young women asked for a light from their young women friends; some had the shadow of a shared childhood between them. The middle-aged were coupled, mainly to their present partner or to a silent vibration of their past one, a fretful wind in the fields within their eyes.

The chatter continued. A number of things were funny. A number of things were not. God was thanked every couple of minutes. Then an ex was brought up. Throughout, as if continuously lining the scene with glue so it wouldn't break, were the Indian rose sellers. They made their way through the people holding wide bouquets of red and white roses. Person by person, a rose was offered.

(These rose sellers are unaffected by the phrase "No, thank you." They find each person's eyes, tilt forward their bouquet and, like a monk, chant their limitless belief in each individual's need for a rose, just one, white or red, with or without the plastic, two euros... He'll wait, he'll wait a lifetime for the realization to come: the rose and how you needed it.)

2

The domed roof of the church across the street seemed to watch over the bar with an ancient grin. Inside, down the cold corridor, there was an open space with glimmers of violet and emerald and gold on the floor from the stained-glass window. Above, in the balcony overlooking the podium, the pipes of the grand organ sat like wolves' teeth. On the other side of the bar, next door, an optician's store stood dim.

A train track ran underneath the church and the bar and the optician's store. A train passed every four to six minutes, from the train station, Gare de l'Est. The metal rails buzzed after one passed. Their hum was absorbed by the lacquered wooden floorboards of the church and the floor tiles of the optician's and the dull, dark rubber flooring of the bar. Every four to six minutes, the hum rose.

3

On the terrace, a long-stemmed white rose was being pulled out of a bouquet. Jean-Luc placed a two-euro coin into the rose seller's palm.

"Merci," said the Indian rose seller, as if revealing the truth.

4

Inside the bar, the elevated stage was lit from various angles, leaving the wires taped to the floor in the dark. From the rear of the stage, three steps led down to the back door. Like the wall, like the stairs, like the floor, it was painted all black.

The drummer and the double bass player were nodding to the rhythm they were playing. The pianist ran his fingers effortlessly over the keys and closed his eyes and bent his head forward.

5

Inside the bar, from the front table, Jean-Luc watched Béatrice. As she ended a verse, his lips mumbled in echo, "*Do-bee do-bee doo…"* Emmanuelle wedged her hand into his. He turned to her and she smiled at him nervously. He knew his cue. He put his arm around her. Emmanuelle settled into his hold and returned to watching her sister. But something kept distracting her. A woman in a wheelchair was outright staring at her Béatrice, and Béatrice seemed to be staring right back.

6

The song finished and the applause went off like a room full of mouse traps. Sabine took her folded hands off the dark blue leather purse on her lap and raised them up. They parted and stretched open in front of her face. Then, her palms snapped together. Between each clap her eyes remained locked onto Béatrice's face.

7

Béatrice had noticed the woman as soon as she appeared amidst the rows of other people, most of whom were sitting, but not in wheelchairs.

You. Sabine's eyes seemed to say. *Me, yes*, Béatrice knew. But she was no longer the flat-chested little girl in the dunes. She had a straight back and buoyant, ample breasts that everyone could agree were very, very nice to look at. Béatrice pinched a smile and matched the woman's glare.

8

*You…*Sabine's eyes repeated, over and over again, like waves coming onto the shore. As everyone clapped and shifted in their seats, the two women held each other's gaze. Sabine was not trying to intimidate Béatrice. Or establish a hierarchy. All of that was left behind in the dunes. There, the roles played out ceaselessly, beyond the two women the girls had become. *Go ahead,* Béatrice dared.

9

"Do-bee do-bee doo..." The tune sounded like the beginning of Frank Sinatra's "Strangers in the Night."

10

Beneath the table, Jean-Luc rolled the stem of a white rose in his palm. With the other hand, he squeezed Emmanuelle's shoulder.

11

Prestadas cosas nos poseen. "Borrowed things posses us," the woman says as if to herself as she brushes the girl's hair. The girl's eyes are still scanning the crack in the wall. Now she is watching Béatrice on stage, one hand holding the microphone, the other smoothing over her blonde chignon.

12

Sabine's chin began to drop and her eyes rolled down to her lap. She pressed them closed for a moment, and when they opened again, they were glossy and wounded. Her mouth softened and her lips parted, as her cheekbones began to rise and form a word without sound.

"*Na-ta-sha,*" she mouthed at Béatrice.

13

Emmanuelle couldn't place the woman's face, but something of her looked familiar. She wanted to get a better look, but knew it was rude to stare at people in wheelchairs, so she turned back to face the stage. The lights were already dimming on her sister's face for the interval. When Emmanuelle turned back towards the woman in the wheelchair, she was already being wheeled away by a slim man with a bruised face, her carer maybe. She watched them, hoping the woman would turn around to get one more glimpse of her sister. But it was the man who turned around, putting his face straight in a ray of spotlight. His bloated nose and puffed eyes almost made Emmanuelle jump.

14

Sabine reached back, found César's arm and pulled on his wrist. César leaned in.

"We are done with our walk now. Take me home."

"Um—okay, sure. You're the boss," César replied.

As César prepared to maneuver the wheelchair around, he thought he heard Sabine say something back, but her voice was eaten up by the noise in the bar. He assumed she had said something upright and stiff like "Yes, I'm the boss" or "Let's go," but all Sabine had really said was "Thank you."

15

Jean-Luc turned back to see what Emmanuelle was looking at.

"What a guy, huh. It's as if he's wheeling that lady around 'til he breaks down and they switch places..." he said.

Emmanuelle did not laugh. Jean-Luc kissed her cheek.

"What's the matter, kitten..."

"Meow, meow," Emmanuelle said in return.

"Does that man scare you?"

"Meow, meow..."

"Oh, don't be frightened, I won't let him eat you up."

"Meow, meow," Emmanuelle murmured and nudged her head into Jean-Luc's shoulder. Her father looked over, and gave Emmanuelle a hearty wink. He liked seeing Emmanuelle in Jean-Luc's arms, like a piece of melting cheese. So different from his other daughter, who always seemed to harden at the touch of others.

Emmanuelle did not see her father's wink because in that instant, the warmth of Jean-Luc's body made her eyes close. And when her eyes closed, there came the image of the woolen man. And when they opened, there was her father, waving his hand at her. Emmanuelle meant to tell her father to stop waving because he was scaring her just then, but instead she accidentally said again, "Meow, meow."

16

Béatrice's eyes followed the woman in the wheelchair as the slim man pushed her through the crowd.

(The little blonde girl stood with her hands clasped at her chest, her toes clutching the sand. She watched the girl with two tight chestnut braids falling through the years.)

César wheeled Sabine out the door.

17

Beneath the applause, Béatrice made her way towards the back door. She walked carefully away from the light, holding the side of her dress. No matter how she moved her feet, they seemed to walk to the same rhythm: *Na-ta-sha.*

At the edge of the stage, Béatrice took three steps down to the backroom door. *Na-ta-sha.* In the fading claps, her hand reached for the door. She pushed it open. Béatrice took one step inside, then another, then another. *Na-ta-sha.*

18

The door shut behind her. The corridor was illuminated by a series of coin-sized lights on the ceiling. Their feeble light, like a breath in winter, hovered over Béatrice's head, but did not help her see. She reached out against the corridor wall and walked slowly, feeling for the main light switch. She remembered it being on the right side, at the level of her hip, a couple of steps from the door, but now she couldn't seem to find it. Her fingertips grazed over and over the wall.

Her hand stopped. Beyond the sound of her fingers on the wall was another sound, thick and dull like rubber. Extending her neck forward, she listened to the fog of voices on the other side of the door. Their sound seem to be waning, as if they were being carried off somewhere. The noise persisted, thick and dull, like everyone in the bar holding their breath. Béatrice waited, expecting to hear a mouth fall open and a gust of wind to surge out. She waited, but no one gasped for air on the other side.

The hand which was not touching the wall came up to her ear. The fingers touched around her earlobe, then pressed on the skin behind the ear. That's where it was, Béatrice realized. The sound, like rubber. It was not coming from the outside, but from inside her own head.

Béatrice took a breath and plugged her nose, hoping her ears would pop, but the air bounced back from her cheeks and out of her mouth. Her ears were still full of something. She brought both hands up to her ears and started to rub them. When she put her hands down, they were warm with a sort of static and she felt something opening in her. The breath began to crackle inside her face. Through the crackle, a woman's voice was emerging. Inside her face, the woman was singing:

> *Gracias a la vida que me ha dado tanto*
> *Me dio dos luceros que cuando los abro*
> *Perfecto distingo lo negro del blanco*
> *Y en el alto cielo su fondo estrellado*
> *Y en las multitudes el hombre que yo amo.*

19

The woman's voice sounded like a memory, yet it was no longer coming from inside Béatrice's head. She turned around, but the darkness on one side was identical to the darkness on the other. There was no one there, no one singing.

As she turned back, her head started to feel oddly light. Like a stack of empty envelopes. The song was fading, then it was gone. She reached out to find the light switch, but her fingers did not make contact with the dry wall. They made contact with a warm body, clothed in wool.

"Hello, Miss Playboy," he whispered into the cleared tunnel of her ear.

20

Béatrice's eyes opened wide. The man put a hand over her mouth and the other flat against her back, pushing her completely into him.

She thought her arms must be flailing, like a cartoon tongue in the midst of a scream; she thought her voice was ripping from her vocal chords.

But, in fact, she was holding her breath.

"Sh'relax princess, breedrou yer nose."

21

"Datsagood princess," the man whispered. "I'm gunna take my hand off, but you gotta stay cool and zipped."

Béatrice nodded. The man took his hand off. In the distance, through the wall, she could still hear voices coming from the bar. A laugh, it sounded like her sister's. A string of a voice, something like "yes exactly." Another called out to someone by name. The musicians who accompanied her on stage, where were they now? Chain-smoking on the terrace, already thinking about the next gig.

For a second, she hoped that her family might want to check up on her and go looking in the corridor. But after all the years of pushing them away, telling them to leave her alone, they were trained to keep their distance.

She found the man's eyes in the darkness, two pinheads framed by black wool. "Shh..." the man said into the wool.

His hands were off her now. She could run out the door, into the crowd, laugh like her sister, say "yes, exactly" and call out to someone by name.

Béatrice did none of those things. She stood very still, facing the woolen man, nailed by his pinhead eyes.

22

For a while, neither the man nor Béatrice spoke. Time was passing. No one had come to get her. But surely someone would notice her absence. She was due on stage.

"I have to go," Béatrice said quietly. "I'm the singer, I have to go."

The man did not respond.

"I have to finish singing here."

The man remained silent. His eyes moved over her body, then came back up to her face. Béatrice took a step towards the door. The man mirrored her and blocked her step. She tried again, but the man blocked her again. She couldn't see where his body ended and the emptiness began.

In the darkness, she felt the man's hand rising towards her. She was sure that he was reaching for her neck. This was it. However they name endings, this was it.

Her neck was glowing with expectation. The skin was preparing to be pressed in, to be crumbled. In her throat, the vocal cords pulled taut like elevator ropes.

Béatrice closed her eyes and her eyes stayed open.

23

He touched her. But not on her neck. The woolen man's hands were on her breasts. He squeezed them, one, then the other, one, then the other. Every time his fingers closed in and his palm sucked up her nipple, her stomach flinched. His grip on them grew firmer. He was no longer squeezing, but grabbing her breasts from her. Béatrice gagged. She felt he might pull them off. Her nipples twisted in pain. Her mouth was wide open in terror, but no sound came out.

"Wer playin it cool princess," he said as he continued.

Béatrice nodded.

"You wanna say sumtin?"

Béatrice nodded.

"Okay, bébé, tell me wad you wanna say, butkeep dat voice smood an' low."

Béatrice nodded.

"Smood an' low..." the man repeated.

Béatrice began. She slid the phrase across to the man card by card.

"If...you...want....my...body you should...just...take...it."

The man suddenly took both hands off her breasts. He took a step back so that his pelvis was no longer pressed against her. The tip of his fingers touched the skin of her left temple. He pushed his fingers back over her hair like a brushstroke, and leaned his face in closer to hers. She felt his breath on her cheek.

"Stoopid princessa..." the man whispered. "I don giva shit bout yer body." He leaned in and the wool touched her cheek. "I wan sumting I can take wit me an keep forever."

"...You can keep Miss Playboy forever," Béatrice replied.

XXVI
NO ONE

1

"GIRLS, SOMETIMES I WORRY about you like you're my biological daughters. But none of you are my biological daughters. That's life for you.

"What I mean to say is, despite the fact that some of you are a real sore sight to look at, I think you are all are doing your best to be decent."

The lanky Natasha stands up. "I've been trying really, really hard not to blabber so much 'bout not feeling good."

"Because…" the Head Natasha says.

"Coz…um…no one really likes to hear it."

The Head Natasha's eyes light up.

2

"And what do people like to hear?"

"Um. About how special they are."

"For example…"

"Like…You're a fingerprint, baby!"

"The only one…!"

"…A-a-a rabbit's foot floating in space! …as Einstein would say."

"There is no one like you."

"You're one of a kind…darling."

"Oh! That's nice…'darling'…say it again!"

"Darling…"

"Go on, girls."

"Um."

"Uh."

"…in the whole world—"

"Darling…"

"…in all of time—"

"DARLING."

"…and all the TV channels —"

"There is NO ONE!"

"Like YOU."

The girls pause to think about this.

"…Oh yeah, that does feel pretty good," all the Natashas say together.

XXVII
KITTY-KAT

1

IN THE BACKSTAGE HALLWAY, Béatrice heard piano keys. The percussion was steady. The double bass weaved in. The musicians must have already started without her.

She turned quickly towards the door and grabbed for the handle. The door swung open and she stood squinting into the light. Soon spots and shadows appeared. Then the spots and shadows became people. She looked at the stage. There they were, the musicians, in their places with their backs to her, facing the crowd.

There was the drummer's head keeping his pace.

There was the pianist's wrist hovering near the keys.

There was the bass player tapping one foot.

Then the fourth figure—a curious sight.

There she was. The blonde singer, her back, stiff, upright, covered with black lace to her hairline. The hair was twisted and pinned neatly upon her head. Blonde as the sand.

2

Béatrice watched the blonde singer tilt her head towards the microphone. The singer's hand floated upwards from her side and got lost in front of her body. It held the stand. Her back muscles moved like a slow serpent as she took a breath. Then, just as easy as that, as easy as childhood, as easy as a man's gaze, as easy as a rolling shadow, the woman began to sing.

3

The blonde singer was singing in Béatrice's voice. As the light changed configurations, Béatrice saw a glimpse of the public, just patches of faces, bearded chins, shiny cheeks, and various fragmented grins, floating in the otherwise fuzzy darkness of the bar. The blonde singer let go of the microphone, her hand descended through the open air towards her hip. The white skin of her fingers was glowing. As were the brushed strands on top of her head. As were the borders of her neck. It was then that this black dress appeared not at all decorative, but necessary. A metal lantern for her light.

When Béatrice caught sight of the singer's hand, she thought she saw a cigarette there, burning idly between the woman's fingers. But when she looked again, it was only slow-rising dust in the spotlight.

4

Jean-Luc got up from his chair, keeping his arm close to his side and the white rose against his thigh. He came up to the stage and extended the white rose towards the blonde singer. He looked up and smiled a set of straight, white teeth. The singer looked into his eyes, and her heart melted like hot candle wax. Jean-Luc stood smiling. Natasha was so happy just then she wanted to say, "I told you so!" But to whom? Who would believe such stories.

As she smiled back at Jean-Luc her cheeks began to hollow. Her skin smelled slightly sour. She reached up to run her fingers over her immaculate chignon, but what she found there was stumps of hair, coarse and chopped. Tears began to accumulate in her eyes. They rolled down her cheeks like rain upon a car door.

Not in front of everyone, please, don't take it away from me in front of everyone.

5

Lame body, she'll have to live with, a chorus of women announce.

6

Lame body, she'll have to live with, Béatrice said quietly to herself in the darkness from behind the stage. She watched the blonde singer grow hollow from the inside.

7

Emmanuelle's eyes darted sharply up to the blonde singer on stage. She looked immediately over to her father.

"Aw, honey, don't be jealous…" he father said warmly. "Jean-Luc is just trying to be nice…"

Emmanuelle opened her eyes wide at her father, but could not find the words she wanted to say. She felt Jean-Luc's hand on her shoulder and turned around just as he was taking his seat beside her. "Hey, kitty-kat," he said to Emmanuelle.

Emmanuelle shifted away from Jean-Luc.

"What's the matter…" Jean-Luc said, putting his arm around her.

Emmanuelle flung his arm off her shoulder and darted her eyes to the blonde singer on stage. The father leaned in and said heartily, "You see, son, women are jealous creatures—if you're gunna give one of them a rose, you might as well buy all of them a rose!" The father turned and winked at Emmanuelle.

Emmanuelle tried to shake her head, but only managed a slight rocking motion.

"Is that why you're mad at me, kitty-kat?" Jean-Luc tried to put his arm back around her.

Emmanuelle flung it off again and pointed with her face at the stage. "Okay, okay, mean kitty! If you want, I'll get a rose as well…"

Emmanuelle looked at her mother, who right away put her finger to her lips and said, "Shhh…your sister's singing…"

Emmanuelle wanted desperately to say something, anything, but her whole body suddenly felt empty of words. She pressed her teeth together and looked deeply into Jean-Luc's eyes.

"Don't be sad…I'm going to get you a rose right now." Jean-Luc turned his head around. "I think the rose guy's still there…" He turned back to Emmanuelle. "Which one do you want, kitty-kat…white or red?…Well, hurry up, fussy kitty. He's about to leave. A white one?"

Emmanuelle tried shaking her head again, but now it was rocking up and down.

Before she could do anything else with her head, Jean-Luc was up and making his way to the departing rose seller.

8

Emmanuelle looked back at her sister on stage. She saw a blonde singer, with paper-thin eyes, almost as if drawn on. Her blonde hair seemed to be slipping away from her scalp strand by strand, like cut thread. This thing before her was not her sister, nor any woman. She looked around her at the audience. No one was startled in the least. Then, when her eyes drew back to the stage, she spotted a figure, in the corner by the backstage door. She wanted to call out, "Bee!" but when she opened her mouth, she couldn't make a sound.

9

Béatrice walked effortlessly through the crowd, sliding like water between the spaces of the people. All eyes were on the blonde singer on stage. Only Emmanuelle's head turned, following her real sister's trace through the crowd and out the door.

XXVIII
GRACIAS A LA VIDA

1

As César pulled up by Marcel's apartment, Sabine grabbed the wheels and made the chair stop. "That's fine. You can go."

"You don't want me to take you up?"

"No." Sabine reached for the wheels of her chair.

"I just thought I could take you up and say hi to Marcel."

Sabine turned back to face him. "That's not necessary."

"But…it could be nice. To say hi."

Sabine looked at him without a word.

"Don't you think…" he added.

Her eyes moved away, dismissing him. César bent his knees and knelt down at the side of the chair. He gripped the metal bar.

"The thing is, Marcel's not just my agent, you see he's my… buddy, and I think it'd be…very…nice to say hi."

"Nice things…aren't necessary."

César suddenly looked very childish. His eyebrows bent perplexed and his eyes shone.

"Listen, César the actor, I will tell my father, Marcel the agent, that you were *very, very nice*, if that is what you want…"

César's eyebrows straightened out.

"Really?" he said quietly.

2

Sabine took her hands off her lap and dipped them over the armrests, down to the wheels. The bones were slim and cordially aligned. César was drawn to their dignity. These hands were the hands in old movies, those which inspired replicas in painted wood and plastic and especially marble. These hands should be caressing fox fur or extending an ornate glass towards the light. But instead they were reaching for the dirty rubber tires of a wheelchair.

Watching her use those dignified hands to jerk at the wheels made César very uncomfortable.

3

Don't you recognize yourself... the phrase echoed in César's head.

4

When César was ten, his brothers held him down on a chair in front of the TV screen where a woman had her knees up and her thighs spread. Her pubic hair was completely shaved like a little girl with a slight rash, but when the camera panned up to her chest, she had a pair of full breasts. They bounced as if trying to memorize enthusiasm. Then the camera cut to a close-up of her eyes, closed, lined with mascara, eyelids shimmering with baby blue. Her eyes opened and looked straight at the camera. How old are you, sweetheart? Sweet sixteen. Sour sixty. Satellite six-hundred. *Is that a good age for you?*

That's enough of her eyes, the camera panned down to her mouth. The lips were glossy and rounded. They could have belonged to an infant, one who's worn herself out with all her crying and is now just keeping tempo with a whimper.

Just as the camera was leaving her face, her lips pulled down into a lusty frown, and her own hand, with long red nails on her fingers, slid up her stomach and grabbed onto her own breast. She squeezed and twisted her body. As she was rolling over to her side, she pulled her butt into the camera. Then the angle switched to profile, she was on her spread elbows and knees, like a footstool, and her long hair hanging over her face like a willow tree. She began grinding her body into the emptiness around her.

5

Sometimes Natasha looks very sexy on fotos.

Sometimes she looks like a sad fairytale.

And sometimes she just looks like an ultrasound.

6

Ten-year-old César tensed in his chair as he felt his brothers push in closer behind him. He kept his eyes on the screen, and began to hold his breath. The chair creaked and Raul's hand grabbed the back of César's neck like a claw. His nose was pushed up to the screen, into the girl, whimpering and grinding.

"*No te reconoces?*" Raul whispered into César's ear. "Don't you recognize yourself?"

"CÉSAR EL ACTOR!" Alonzo proclaimed.

7

Sabine jerked the wheels again. As César watched her the memory of the woman in the video from his childhood blurred into Sabine's movements. His eyes felt like the camera, panning up the side of the wheelchair, to her arms, to her lap, where, to his surprise, he now saw a large erect penis that she was holding with one of her stern hands. This hand stroked the penis at a regular pace at first, then accelerated, faster and faster. César wanted to shut his eyes, to look away, but instead, like the camera lens, his eyelids opened wider and zoomed in closer to the fingers gripping down on to the bulging penis. Sabine's hand yanked and yanked at the penis, as César's eyes tried desperately to look away. *Come on, come on, cripple*…a man's voice gritted in his head in the same tone as the porn from his childhood. His eyes slid up and down the penis with her hands. *Come on cripple, get me off!* He saw something inside that penis start to twitch as if it would ejaculate straight into his eyes. Just as the hand gave that penis one final stroke, César shut his eyes and screamed.

"TE MATO, PUTA!"

8

When César opened his eyes again, Sabine had rolled herself up to the door. She turned back to face César.

There was her brow.

There was her jaw.

There was her mouth.

9

Sabine's face was flat and serene. "So…you want to kill me, César the actor?"

César bit on the inside of his lip.

"That's what you would like to do, isn't it…" Sabine continued in a gentle voice. "That's why you want to help me upstairs…You want to show off a bit, isn't that right…you want to kill me in front of Marcel, you want to impress your agent…"

César felt a wind blow across his cheek. He was nodding.

10

"Tell me, César the actor, how would you kill me…?"

César stuffed his hands into his pockets and pulled his shoulders in until he felt covered up.

"Idunno," he mumbled.

"Come on, César, come on, *tell me*…"

"…Idunno. I dunno. Like. Choke you. Maybe."

"I see…And how would you choke me?"

"Idunno…with your own hands."

"Oh. Interesting. And how would you do that?"

"Well…um…on the floor…"

"Mhm…"

"I could…maybe…on top of you. And you could be…under me. And I would hold your wrists against your chest, I guess. Like really tight. And, um…because your legs are…you wouldn't be able to kick or…struggle…you know. You'd just jerk back and forth, like underneath me, but I'd be sitting on your stomach, and I'd be holding your arms down…"

"And where would Marcel be…"

"Marcel could be like, just sitting. At his desk. Like comfortable. Watching."

"I see." Sabine paused for a moment. "César, I have a personal question for you."

"Yeah?"

"I hope you don't find it too rude…"

"No, go ahead…"

"Well, I was just wondering: Would you rape me before or after you killed me?"

11

"…I du*nno*…" His voice cracked.

"Oh, come on now, César."

César lowered his eyes.

"Would you rape me before…or after…you choked me to death with my own hands?"

César continued to look at his shoes.

"Let me help you, César the actor. Let's think about this together, okay? Would you like to put your penis inside of me when I am still jerking around, or would you prefer that your penis enter a more limp, softer body?"

César felt his whole stomach tighten. He pulled one hand out of his pocket and wiped his nose, then stuffed that hand back into his pocket.

"You could, for example, flip me over, and spread my butt cheeks, and put the tip of your penis right up against my anus. It would be squeezed tightly shut, as I would be very frightened. But you could, of course, push your penis in, little by little. That space would be especially tight, so you'd really have to force your way inside. That could be quite nice, no? Pushing your hard penis deeper and deeper into my anus, as my butt cheeks squeeze together around the base because I am so frightened. Also, because you are ripping the tissue around my anus and this is hurting me, in addition to being frightened. But, for you, it must feel really nice, to push your penis into that warm, tight space…It would, wouldn't it…It would feel really, really nice…"

César sniffed again. A drop hit his shoe.

"Stopit," he mumbled.

"You're an actor, aren't you, César, hm? Isn't that so? Well ACT, then, ACT, César, ACT!"

César couldn't speak. He couldn't look up. He couldn't even pull his hands out of his pockets to wipe the blood dripping from his nose. Then, beneath the tapping of the droplets of blood on his shoe, he heard a creaking sound. He lifted his head and saw Sabine with her back to him, shifting her position in the wheelchair. She was suddenly no longer concerned with him. Her arms were straightening out, as her hands gripped the armrests. In one elegant gesture, both arms swiftly pushed Sabine up to her feet. She typed in the building's entry code and stepped neatly over the metal door frame. The door thumped shut behind her and the empty wheelchair rolled back on to César's feet.

12

César stood alone in the street. His pants felt tight. He took both hands out of his pockets and looked down. His penis was hard. Suddenly embarrassed, he darted his head around to see if there was anyone else in the street as he tried to adjust himself. No one, good. But as he looked back down, he saw that it had grown even bigger. It was bulging painfully against his zipper. He immediately hunched over himself, trying to hide it, to soften it, but could feel his erection continue to get harder and fatter. In his hunched position, he tugged at his pants, left, right, out, down, trying desperately to calm this thing down. But the more he twisted, the more it seemed to grow. Now he was afraid to look down. He could feel this hard-on ballooning out of him. His neck was straining. His cheeks were burning. César closed his eyes, begging to be relieved from it all. In his darkness, his arms and legs tangled, and he tripped and fell onto his knees. When his full weight hit the cement, César let out such a deep, pitting cry, that it echoed backwards through all his lived years and pinched his mother's womb.

13

When César opened his eyes, a dark silhouette of a man stood before him. The man extended his black leather-gloved hand towards César and César took it and stood up in one simple motion. The dark silhouette leaned in and kissed César on the lips.

The man then slid his woolen cheek against César's and whispered into his boyish ear, "*Bravo, mi amor.*"

XXIX
THE LOUVRE

1

"Excuse me…"

"Yes?"

The Head Natasha stops her lesson and looks down at the crouching girl.

"Um…I was just wondering…"

"Yes…"

"…where does our *pain* go?"

She takes her arms off her knees and sits up. Her kneecaps look like two putrid papayas.

2

"Well, that is a good question. You see, whatever hurts on your body is like a mass of cold water rising and breaking against a bunch of rocks, and you just have to remember that there's someone up there with a paintbrush and easel, trying very hard to paint every droplet of that crash onto a canvas, so you can't be moving around too much. If you stay still, he can finish the painting, and then it can be hung up in the Louvre."

"*Loov-rah*," the Natashas repeat.

"And that's where it goes, girls. It becomes a PAINting."

3

I said, trees take my scream. I said, soil, take my scream. I said water, take my scream, a chorus of women chant.

4

One Natasha yawns. "My soul hurts…"

5

"Louv-rah."

XXX
LOUV-RAH

1

BÉATRICE WALKED DOWN THE streets unnoticed. She strolled down
the canal, past the lingering picnickers, past the bars, past the closed
shops.

She walked south, all the way down to Place de la Bastille,
where the prison was stormed and the French Revolution took
fire.

She turned west and walked away from the former prison, which
now was a glimmering roundabout, enclosed by banks, various cin-
emas, sushi shops, candy stores, restaurant chains, gelato counters,
bars, and the Bastille Opera House, where the particles of human an-
guish and Godly intervention rested like dust upon the closed mouths
of the folded audience seats.

She walked for a while on Rue de Rivoli, where some couples
sat on the curb arguing and others stood against the door kissing,
and flocks of men regrouped around women, and people asked
each other for cigarettes with slight slurs, smelling of sugar and
rum.

She walked past the shop where she had found her dress. The
windows were empty now and the door had a sign: PROPERTY
FOR SALE.

2

Béatrice walked until there was no one else on the streets. Cars drove by. She felt each one approaching from behind, its headlights touching her heels. With each car, she thought, this is the one. This is the one which will pull up at my side. This is the car with the car door that will open for me. Inside will be the man who will extend his arm towards me. That arm will be for me, only me. That arm will grab my body and pull me in. This will be the car which will take me east, out of Paris, out of France—to that highway with the low metal barrier, behind which is the sparse forest with the wet soil, and the bent speed limit sign, and the empty liquor bottles, and the chewed-up panties, and the broken nails...

(Hey, I know that highway...Go one way and you're in Dresden... Go the other way and you're in Prague...)

(The problem's the in-between.)

The light touches Béatrice heels, then climbs her calves, thighs, and races up her back.

(Keep walking, Béatrice.)

3

Cars passed her one after the other. To her left, the wall of the Louvre, beige-gray stone. As she walked, she glanced up at the high, arched windows. They were covered with thin white curtains, so one could not see inside. Behind them, hidden from the pedestrians, were marble-floored hallways. These hallways led to a series of square, windowless rooms, one opening into another. On the walls of these square rooms, paintings hung like military service ribbons.

From the street, though, as Béatrice was walking, all she could see was the row of tall and narrow arched windows covered in white gauze like recovering eyes, the lower row with bars across the windows. If she hadn't known this was the Louvre, she might have thought it was a prison.

She drew her gaze away, back to the grandiose street stretching out before her and the burnt blue skyline framed by the Haussmann buildings, balconies laced with black bars, stonework ridges studded with medallions, mansard roofs, flat-faced and monumental.

(Keep walking, Béatrice.)

4

She could have turned at Pont-Neuf and gone to the Seine and jumped in it. That would have been something. But she didn't. She kept on walking alongside the Louvre wall, one street lamp after the other, one barred window after another, until she reached the gate she needed to reach. Lucky for her it was open. The gate was tall with black spires, the top spikes painted gold. Béatrice passed under the archway, walked through the hallway to the second pair of gold-tipped gates, which were incidentally also open. She walked through them and into that noble courtyard.

5

The courtyard contained four glass pyramid structures. One large pyramid in the center, which, during working hours, served as the entrance for patrons, and three smaller ones on each side. The smaller glass pyramids were divided by dark marble pools where, after sundown, water ran like black silk.

The pyramids were surrounded like a barracks by ornate ledges, populated with various statues: mostly a lot of fools, foolish Gods, foolish humans.

There was a sort of eternal laugh that seemed to be vibrating from all of them. It just barely tickled the scalp. That wasn't the only thing that was emitting a vibration. Béatrice looked to the left and saw that one small glass pyramid was glowing.

6

As she approached it, she felt its glow. She reached out and touched the warm glass. She put both her palms on a glass panel and leaned forward to look inside.

7

The lights were on. There were two short escalators, both at a standstill. Across from them, a marble counter with a sign "audio guide." At this hour, there was no one behind the counter. Against the wall were two racks where the audio-guide headsets hung like rows of shoelaces. In front, metal stands marked out a stretched lane for the waiting line, still trying to keep order in the emptiness.

Next to the corner of the counter, before the escalators, there was a wide marble bowl with a tree planted in it. Béatrice walked around the side of the glass pyramid, drawn to see more of this oddly placed tree, when something stopped her. She leaned into the glass until her nose touched the transparent surface. There, between the audio-guide station, the potted tree and the escalators, was a woman, completely naked, lying on the ground.

8

The naked woman's skin was very similar to the floor, marbled in different shades. Béatrice might not have seen her if it hadn't been for the meshes of brown hair that fell in waves from her head. The woman's knees were up, leaning into each other. Her arms were crossed over her face. They rested upon her brow in the form of a clean *X*. Perhaps she was shielding herself, from the light, or from all that open space around her flesh. Despite her position, she was not resting. Something about her was quite alert. Her bellybutton peered out like an insomniac eye.

9

The woman arched her back and shifted her knees, then uncrossed her arms and looked up at Béatrice. Her eyebrows were dark strokes, her eyes wide and waiting.

10

"…Polina…" Béatrice called down.

11

Polina's lips began to curl into a smile. As it rose, Béatrice's mouth mirrored from above.

With the same inhale, both women's lips parted. Together, they breathed out. One from inside the glass pyramid and one from outside. Their breath joined on the glass panel.

12

From the glass, their breath peeled off and floated freely upward. It reached the stone and marble of the Louvre, then passed into the courtyard, through the foolish statues, and up into the cavernous evening.

It continued higher and higher, passing by aeroplanes taking sleepy passengers back to France. It floated away from Europe, above the continents.

It left the stratosphere and was brushed by hurrying meteors. There it floated by orbiting traces of animals which had been sent into space out of human curiosity. It sifted through the particles of Laika the dog, and Albert I and II, the monkeys, and the garden spider Arabella, and the pair of Japanese tree frogs.

Now Polina's and Béatrice's breath was made up of all these things. Stone dust, avalanches, Arabella's legs. It joined a certain low humming of billions of voices. It took its place among all of these voices, and was at home everywhere.

13

*Do-bee do-bee doo…*all the voices hummed. A pair of legs began to spread and the room filled with applause.